THE LOST OPAL

PATTY WISEMAN

Books by Patty Wiseman

Velvet Shoe Collection
An Unlikely Arrangement
An Unlikely Beginning
An Unlikely Conclusion
An Unlikely Deception
An Unlikely Elegance

Success Your Way

That One Moment
Somewhere Between
Silver's Redemption
The Lost Opal

Rescue At Wiseman's Pond

Book Liftoff
1209 South Main Street
PMB 126
Lindale, Texas 75771

Printed in the United States of America
Wiseman, Patty
The Lost Opal / Patty Wiseman.
Fantasy—Romance—Fiction.2. Contemporary—Romance—Fiction.
BISAC: FIC027020 FICTION / Romance / Contemporary.
FIC009090 FICTION / Fantasy / Romance
First Edition.
ISBN: 978-1-947946-83-5
ISBN: 978-1-947946-84-2

www.pattywiseman.com
www.bookliftoff.com

I want to dedicate this book to my husband, Ron. He's always got my back, stands ready with encouragement, explores ways to make it all happen.

If I need anything he is johnny on the spot to provide it. After almost thirty years of marriage, he is the partner I was meant to be with, the one who holds my hand as I navigate through the health issues I've had to conquer, the one who puts himself last in order that I might thrive.

I'm blessed to have him as a partner in life.

THE LOST OPAL

CHAPTER ONE

THE ODD HIGH-PITCHED SOUND, NOT UNLIKE A WOMAN'S cry, drifted in from the water as thirty-year-old book illustrator Maren Raybourn stared out to sea. She searched for the source of the eerie call, one hand shading her eyes as the late afternoon sun dipped lower. The electrified wind caused her long, blonde hair to swirl around her face.

Must be my imagination or I'm overly tired. Sure don't need something weird to take me away from my work. She shivered and turned to resume tending the first clambake of the season, or at least, that's what the locals told her. The Pacific Northwest remained chilly in spring, especially on this part of the coast. No warm sandy beaches on this ocean.

A steady heat radiated from the large rocks in the deep, freshly dug hole ready to receive the bounty. Maren rubbed both hands together over the warmth of the pit and whispered, "I'm grateful my nosy neighbor Josh taught me how to do a proper clam bake. Time to put that information into practice. Wonder if I could incorporate this experience into a children's book?"

The first order of business was to rake the coals from the fire and lay seaweed on the steaming rocks. Next, she placed the clams, potatoes, and corn into the wire baskets.

The only thing left to do is cover them with more seaweed and pull the tarp over the whole thing.

After a step back to survey the finished product, she contemplated Josh and his eagerness to secure their friendship. His cabin was up the beach to the right. He made himself a nuisance with constant visits and invitations to dinner or a movie. She came here to finish the illustrations for the children's book per her contract. The deadline was less than a week away and she didn't want to be distracted. He convinced her it was expected of her as the newbie to invite the surrounding neighbors for this clambake. No amount of protest convinced him otherwise, so she gave in to shut him up, but made a mental note to have a serious talk with him.

The foamy waves beat a never-ending cadence against the rocky shore which prompted her to speak aloud as she enjoyed the rhythm, "The atmosphere is so peaceful here. I could listen to the ocean's serenade forever. My rowdy neighbors will shatter the quiet all too soon, though. Best get the rest of the gear down here." She hiked toward the beach house but stopped and turned. "What is that?"

Once more, a sound pierced the tranquil landscape, mournful and sad. At the edge of the water, a shimmering mirage danced beside an immense edifice everyone dubbed Passion Rock.

She called out. "Hello? Who are you?" Maren shaded her eyes again and marched toward the sight. The closer she got, the more the illusion faded, until it disappeared into the restless sea.

On the shoreline, she searched around the boulder for signs of the strange apparition. She poked a stick at the soil, touched the rough, cold surface of the huge rock, and leaned against it to study the sea. The only thing in her view was the rhythmic back and forth of the waves. Nothing had disturbed the wet, gritty sand, only her own imprints.

A male voice shattered the silence. "Maren, where are you? You're supposed to be minding the fire."

Her pulse raced at the disturbance but slowed in relief at

the familiar voice. She smiled at the six foot, red-headed beach bum. She waved. "Hey Josh, you're early. Thought I heard something…a high-pitched sound. Guess my overactive imagination got the best of me. There was a sort of mirage dancing on the water, too."

When she glanced back at the water's edge, the mirage was gone. She sprinted toward him trying to shake the unease in the pit of her stomach and rubbed her arms to dispel the goose bumps.

Josh glanced around the camp. "Did you find anything?" He stopped at the pit and lifted the canvas. "Wow, this smells amazing. I'm starved."

"Put that down, it's gonna be another hour. Come to the house and help me with the rest of the food." She grabbed his arm and pulled him toward the cabin.

"You didn't answer me. Did you find anything?" The screen door banged shut behind them, and Josh headed to the kitchen.

The counter displayed the remainder of the feast, various bags of chips, condiments, a veggie plate. While she hurried to gather the items, she continued to talk of the apparition. "No— have you ever heard a funny sound down here? It kinda spooked me. Mermaids don't exist, but if I didn't know better…"

He caught the plastic butter container as it slipped out of Maren's arms. "You gonna carry everything yourself? Why did you drag me up here?"

"Sorry, thinking about the mermaid thing. Grab the basket with the drinks."

He did as he was told. "To answer your question, yes, I've sensed the sound. Wasn't sure the noise was real. Thought it was my imagination, too. Never could trace it to anything. Could be a spy ship off the coast or something. You know, sonar…submarine." He held the door open for Maren with one foot.

The short walk to the picnic site gave her a moment to think.

"That would explain the sound, but I saw a shiny object dancing on the water. Any clues?" She unfolded a beach chair and flopped down to catch her breath.

"Optical illusion. Happens all the time." He arranged his chair close to the steaming food. "It'll be dark soon. The mysterious mirage might make an appearance."

Welcoming shouts filled the air.

"Hey, here's the rest of the gang." Maren put the odd incident out of her mind and focused on the clambake.

The pressure of the city seemed far away as the group gathered. Here, she could unleash creativity, finish the book illustrations with a calm soul. When she first arrived at the beach, she'd wanted to be completely alone, but eventually, the other residents sought her out and all but forced her into the social climate.

Josh introduced his buddy Nick, who stayed in town to be closer to his job.

"Glad you could come, Nick. Grab a chair." She pointed toward the beach chairs.

The next to arrive were Lulu and Annie. They shared a cabin on the far side of hers.

"Hey ladies, the food is ready when you are."

That left Rose, a loner who lived a few cabins down.

"Happy to have you, Rose. Bottled drinks are in the cooler over there." She indicated the direction close to the table.

No one dated; they were all simply pals, beach bums, plain and simple. Oh, everyone had jobs, but any down time was spent right here on the waterfront, and through shear persistence they pulled Maren into the circle.

In the middle of the clams, corn-on-the-cob, and lively conversation, the newest member of their small group, quiet, beautiful, auburn-haired Rose Clancy, spoke for the first time. "Have you witnessed the call of the sea sylph since you arrived last week, Maren?"

Silence fell over all six picnic-goers.

Maren swallowed the clam whole. "Sea sylph—what do you mean? A…mermaid?" She hadn't mentioned the illusion to the others and a quick glance at Josh, who shrugged his shoulders, assured her he hadn't either.

"I guess you could say that. More like an apparition, though—or so the story goes. I'm guessing you haven't heard it. You will eventually…it's legend down here." Rose wrapped a shiny curl around her finger and glanced around. She then recited a haunting rhyme, her voice in singsong so melodious everyone sat in rapt attention and hung on every word.

'Beware the siren's song of the sea,
Lest you're drawn like moth to flame.
For one mistake will require the key
To restore a soul from whence it came'

The path to freedom is in her smile,
A bright twinkle in her eye.
A portal key reveals her guile,
So the fetters you can untie.

'Beware, do not look to the view,
Only your heart can stop the fall.
For the siren hides a secret clue,
In plain sight but hidden from all.'

A chill settled over Maren's skin, turning the smoothness into goose bumps once more. *Her eyes…they're the color of black-berry wine when the fire light hits them. And how does Rose know this so-called folklore? Josh said she only arrived a few days ago.*

"There's a legend? I did hear a funny sound today, a high-pitched, sad, moan-type call."

Rose sat upright and pointed a finger at her. "That's it! No problem, of course…unless you see the shimmering wraith. If you ever see it, run like hell." She settled back in the beach chair and continued to stare at her hostess.

Everyone rattled off questions and demands for the newcomer to tell the tale in the cool, moonlit night.

The air turned arctic despite the heavy, wool sweater Maren wore. She held her breath as Rose gave an account of the so-called legend of Passion Rock.

"I was told the fable as a girl, but never desired to find out more—scared the daylights out of me. My family loved coming here when I was a child. You're lucky I even showed up here tonight, especially so close to that thing." She pointed toward the ocean. "Anyway, myth says a ship wrecked off this beach during the war with the British. The captain was rescued by an auburn-haired beauty who lived here…in the very cabin you reside in now, Maren. They fell in love. He vowed, when the war was over, to return and claim their life together. Years later he did come back, but she was gone. The locals say she succumbed to the ocean, lonely and delirious from waiting."

"She drowned herself?" Josh asked, gaze riveted on Rose.

"So they say. No one found any trace of her, ever. The tale goes on to say she'll return to claim her lost love, her captain."

The evening passed with speculations about the validity of the folk lore. It made for intriguing conversation, like ghost stories around a campfire. She decided that's all it was, a ghost story designed to scare everyone to death, and deftly steered the discussion to the local band, *The Beachcomers*. They played in the town on weekends.

By midnight, the party ended, and one by one, they drifted off to their own homes. Except Rose.

Maren refused Josh's offer to stay the night to 'save' her

from the ghostly appearance, and he finally wandered off with the others.

The two women carried the last of the food into the house.

Maren had to ask. "Why did you stay behind? You have a long walk home alone. I'm sure someone would have walked with you. After all, there's the legend and all. You said the story creeps you out."

Rose set the clam-laden platter down on the butcher block island. "I watched your face when I told the story —you saw her."

"Something…I saw something." She skirted around Rose, uncomfortable with her closeness. "Didn't look like a woman or a mermaid. It was shiny and kind of vibrated. The closer I got, the farther away the thing went, until it was out in the water, and gone." She motioned for her guest to sit on the sofa. "So, what does it mean?"

Rose shook her head at the offer. "Thanks, but I can't stay. Be warned. She comes at first spring, and they say the woman who bears the name of the sea will take her place."

"Take her place? Please explain and how do you know so much about it?"

"Not sure of the meaning…that's how the myth goes. I spent summers on the beach as a child, that's when I first became aware of the story. You might ask some of the locals. They say she will find her captain again, but he will be punished for abandoning her." Rose moved toward the door. "Thanks for the food and fellowship. Next time we'll do it at my place." She gave her a quick hug and sprinted out the door.

Rose's willowy frame disappeared into the night. Maren remained on the porch staring after her, muttering, "The woman who bears the name of the sea…"

After only thirty minutes in the rumpled sheets, she sat straight up. The niggling feeling in the back of her mind finally surfaced. "Maren…my own name. I wonder what it means?" Despite the frosty air, she climbed out from beneath her cozy comforter and padded barefoot to the desk.

The laptop powered up and ten fingers flew across the keys to find the definition of the name Maren. "Star of the Sea. Wow," she breathed.

Dressed only in her favorite short, pink cotton nightdress and a heavy wool sweater, she wandered out on the deck and watched the waves pulsate in and out from the shore. The night smelled of salt water, and the spray moistened her skin as she descended the stairs and strolled toward the water, still talking out loud. "Nonsense—it's only a story, a myth. I didn't really see anything. The sound could have been as Josh said…sonar. Was Rose trying to scare the new kid on the block? My name…well, dad named me, and he was a sailor, so the name is perfectly normal, a coincidence."

Movement near the enormous rock captured her attention. She stepped closer.

"Out rather late, aren't we, miss?" A deep male voice asked.

The accent triggered a familiar chord, a slight Scottish brogue, but she couldn't place it until she turned around abruptly. The resemblance to a young Sean Connery, right down to the dimples and cocked eyebrow, took her breath away.

Reflex caused a quick flutter of hands to cover her skimpy attire. She found her voice quickly. "For Pete's sake, you scared the life out of me. Do you always sneak up on people in the middle of the night? Who are you?"

"I apologize. Habit. I always take a midnight stroll on the beach each night. I've never encountered you out at this hour—thought you might be sleepwalking. The way you are dressed and all….” He averted his magnetic dark eyes and feigned a sweeping bow. “The name is Drake Morgan, at your service.”

She hurried up the porch steps. “Well, Mr. Morgan, I’m sorry, but I wasn’t sleepwalking.” The screen banged shut.

“That’s *Captain* Drake Morgan,” he shouted at the closed door.

The lock settled into place at a twist of her wrist, and her hand froze on the metal bolt. In a low voice she said, “Did he say Captain? Am I walking in my sleep? Now, I’ve imagined I met a captain in the middle of the night.”

A peek through the white, gauze curtain on the door window proved he wasn’t a figment of her imagination.

He continued down the beach. *Back to his house, I suppose. Too many stories, too many odd occurrences, and now a strange man. It’s all a dream…or a bad clam. I’m going back to bed.*

CHAPTER TWO

A FITFUL NIGHT AND A STORM BREWING OFFSHORE DIDN'T improve Maren's mood the next morning. As she stretched and yawned, she announced to the empty kitchen, "I need coffee. I'd feel better if the sun would shine today."

She dressed in her favorite distressed jeans and a red T-shirt, and with a steaming mug in hand moved to the studio in the sunroom. The large windows let in an abundance of light and generated warmth on chilly days.

The caffeine kicked in, and the artwork left from the day before consumed the morning. Deadlines were her forte, a real motivator. She concentrated on the colors, making sure they blended well. Proud of the finished product, she held it to the light and admired her handiwork, three puppies romping in the trees with a fawn watching nearby. She reached for the phone to call her editor, but a rap on the door interrupted the call.

"Miss…it's me, Captain Morgan, or Drake if you prefer. I'd like to talk to you." His knock was soft, hesitant.

The phone dropped into the cradle. *The man on the beach last night? What could he want?* Her keychain lay on the table, and she grabbed it as she walked by. If she pushed the button, her blue Buick Encore would sound the alarm. *Can't be too careful.*

The door blew open at her touch. "What is it? I'm working."

He looked down at her hand with the key chain. "I don't

want to be a bother. After last night, I thought an apology, in the light of day, was in order. Like a…good neighbor policy. Didn't mean to scare you. You never gave me your name, either. I like to become acquainted with all the folks on this beach." A paper grocery bag nestled inside the curl of his elbow. "I brought breakfast."

His well-worn captain's hat sat askew, and black curls tumbled from underneath its brim. She couldn't help but smile at his crooked grin and the twinkle in those striking brown eyes. Her first instinct was to slam the door in his face, but his smile warmed her heart. "Well, I'm working, but I can use breakfast. I tend not to feed myself on a regular basis. Alright, come in."

As he took command of the kitchen he said, "You can put the keys down. I'm not a stalker."

The aroma of scrambled eggs and bacon filled the kitchen as Drake exhibited excellent culinary skills. "There you are milady…breakfast fit for a princess."

"Smells wonderful, but I only asked you in here for one reason." The eggs melted in her mouth. She reached for another bite.

"Let me guess…my boyish good looks?"

"No, I want to hear about the legend." The fork hung in mid-air as she waited for a reaction.

Drake's face darkened; the easy smile gone. "Whoa, you don't beat around the bush, do you? Questions like, how long have you lived here, Drake, what kind of a captain are you, are you a serial killer? That line of questioning never entered your mind?"

"Just answer the question. Do you know about the legend— oh, and what kind of a captain are you?" She wagged the empty fork at him.

"Legends are for dreamers. I'm aware of the story, but don't take any stock in it. Why?"

He took the last bite of breakfast and scooped his plate and utensils to the sink.

The dishes clanged, and the running water almost drowned out the question.

His clipped tone suggested he didn't want to talk about it, and after a short consideration, she shrugged, "I hear noises. High pitched sounds. I've seen mirages on the water, also."

He answered in a hurried tone. "A natural phenomenon. Happens in the spring. Some kind of atmospheric event, kind of like the aurora borealis lights. Trust me; it's not the mermaid legend."

His own dishes finished, he swept up her empty plate, washed and dried the remainder, hung up the towel, and walked quickly toward the door. "Thanks for allowing me to make up for scaring you last night. I live four houses down. Come by anytime. I'll make dinner for you. Gotta go."

"Wait," she hollered. "You didn't tell me what kind of a captain you are."

"I was in the Navy for ten years. Now, I captain a yacht tour boat called *Sea Star*. I'm on hiatus until the new season opens up." He touched his cap and was gone.

She waved and watched him until he disappeared down the beach. *Sea Star. Wow, that's interesting.* Her voice was drowned by the roar of the ocean as she reflected, "Strange fellow, but nice. Great cook, too. At least he tried to set my mind at ease about the silly mermaid story, but I'm not fooled, he was spooked. Maybe Rose will tell me why. I'm gonna call her."

The phone rang three times. "This is Rose Clancy."

"Hey Rose, do you have a minute? I have a question for you."

"Maren, how are you? Sure, what's up?"

"What do you know about Drake Morgan, the captain?" She tapped the desk with a pencil.

"Drake who? Never heard of him. Did you meet a guy? How cool, tell me about him."

The pencil clattered to the floor. "I thought you knew

everyone on the beach. He's four houses down from mine. Captain Drake Morgan. Don't mess with me; just tell me about him."

"Honest, I don't know him. By the way, no one lives in the house you describe. It's run down and has been abandoned for a while now. Are you okay? You sound funny. Do you want me to come…"

The phone slipped slightly from her ear. She dropped into the wicker chair by the worktable, and whispered out loud, "Alright, I've had enough. You are a grown woman, Maren. You don't believe in myths and legends. It's a joke, that's all." She leaped up, hung up the telephone, forgetting Rose was still on the line, and stomped to the studio. "I'm being set up. This beach idea was a mistake. I'm heading back to the city at the end of the month."

≫✦≪

The conversation with her editor the next morning left her apprehensive. Things were getting sticky in the city. Her job was actually at risk if she didn't finish the illustrations on time. The editor/publisher urged her to stay there and complete her work. She wasn't happy about it but agreed.

Josh stopped by mid-morning and caught her on the deck daydreaming, focusing on the beach toward the captain's cabin. "I thought you were supposed to be working, Maren. Isn't that why you've spurned all my advances? Now, I catch you staring into space." He bounded up the stairs. "Am I being brushed off?"

Her concentration was so complete she didn't see him approach and bumped her leg on the patio table at the unexpected sound of his voice. "Good grief, Josh. Would it hurt to warn a girl?" Embarrassed, she rubbed her knee.

"Hey, I made plenty of noise coming up. Your mind was

pretty far away." His glance darted down the beach. "What's so interesting?"

"Have you met Drake Morgan? Captain Morgan?" she asked.

The chair he flopped into scraped across the deck with his weight. "I think someone told me about a handsome dude moving into a cabin down the way. I haven't been introduced." He frowned. "Is that what's got your attention? A hot new guy?"

She turned and went inside to hide the heat rising up her neck. "Not at all. He stopped by late the other night. No one had mentioned him before, so I was curious, that's all." *He doesn't need to know Morgan fixed me breakfast.*

The chagrined redhead followed her. "Hey, these drawings are wonderful. Never considered you were really that talented. Are these for children's books?"

"Yeah, and I have a deadline, so you should skedaddle. I've work to do." She held the door open and nodded toward the beach.

"Okay, okay, I get the message. Just came by to ask if you wanted to go into town for a bite to eat. I understand when I'm being booted."

"Sorry Josh, I just can't take the time, right now. I'm here to work, nothing else."

Try as she might, she couldn't concentrate. Her attention kept wandering toward Captain Morgan's cabin. More than once, she found herself on the deck watching the empty shoreline.

An hour later, she decided to find out for herself. She grabbed a sweater and trudged down the beach hoping to locate the captain's shanty.

It wasn't hard to spot. Just as Rose described, it was a bit run-down, but looked to be occupied. A dark green jeep was parked in the drive and music boomed through the open door. On guard at the front door sat a gigantic, chestnut brown dog, a Bullmastiff to be precise. She knew because her father owned three of them. A low, deep growl rumbled from his chest.

Not one to tempt fate, she turned around and headed back to her own cabin. *That's what I deserve for not sticking to my work. So someone is there, I'm only guessing it must be Drake.*

Her approach slowed at the halfway point. The indecipherable sounds of conversation drifted within earshot. Unfortunately, her eyes were stinging from the chill in the air and refused to focus. *Is there one person or two on my porch?* A woman's laugh carried across the expanse of beach. A lower tone rumbled along with it. *A man?*

A second later, the realization dawned she had come to a complete stop. She forced her feet to move forward again. As she came closer, the two forms became distinguishable. Yes…a man and a woman. The female reclined in a wicker chair, while the man stood above her waving his arms in dramatic gesture.

A few more steps and she was sure. It was Josh and Rose. *Why are they on my porch?*

"Hey, you two. I thought I told you to go home, Josh." She rushed forward clutching her sweater tighter around her shoulders.

Rose responded first. "I was worried about you after your phone call. I decided to come and see for myself after you didn't return my call. He was telling me you grilled him about your Captain Morgan, as well?"

"He's not *my* Captain Morgan." She turned toward Josh, again. "And you? What is your excuse?"

He blushed. "I came to ask you one more time to dinner, before you leave."

She became annoyed. This was supposed to be a retreat, a place where she could draw in peace, away from the drama of the city. *It appears there is drama everywhere, even here on the beach.*

"Look you two, I have work to do, a deadline to meet. If

you're playing tricks on me for your own amusement, I'm not buying in." She brushed past them both.

Josh stopped and grabbed her arm. "Look, you can't blame a guy for trying. Say, if you're so busy why were you down the beach? Stalking his cabin…curiosity getting the better of you?"

Rose stood and smiled, a mischievous glint dancing in her eye. "Yeah Maren, what were you doing down that far? Spying perhaps?"

A rush of anger overcame her, but she stopped before a reaction surfaced. A deep breath cleansed the rising rancor. "If you insist, yes, I went to see the cabin Rose described to me but was met by a most unfriendly canine. Changed my mind and came back here." She shook off his arm. "Now, I must return to my work."

"Ah, that would be Magnum, his Bullma…" Rose began.

"Yes, Bullmastiff. My father has three of them. Not very friendly. I thought you didn't even know Captain Morgan," she accused. "Something's going on here and I don't like it. Please leave." The screen door banged as she left the two on the deck.

Her throat tightened; tears moistened her eyes. The day had mingled into a swirl of emotions…curiosity, disappointment, and now embarrassment. Drake's cabin certainly succeeded in drawing her away from work, but thankfully, the growling dog sent her packing. No one would have ever found out about her ill-fated plan, but here she was—caught. She was tempted to go back out there and tell them both what she thought, but turned away from the screen, stopped, whirled around, slammed the door, and slid the bolt into place with a bang. The voices faded. She supposed they got the hint and went back to their own abodes.

Now I can get some work done.

CHAPTER THREE

THE NEXT FEW DAYS PASSED IN A QUIET CALM. MAREN MADE considerable progress on the illustrations and lost herself in the work. *Maybe, I can return to the city, after all.*

A mild disappointment nagged her, though. Captain Drake Morgan never returned. She wasn't sure why that fact bothered her. This is what she wanted, to be left alone. And yet…

As the days turned into a week, she caught herself glancing at the phone, looking out the window toward his cabin. Rose hadn't called, either. Even Josh stayed away.

The message she would return on the weekend was delivered to her editor by email, and she started packing. She thought about contacting Josh and Rose to tell them she was leaving, but decided it was best to leave things alone.

Two days before her departure, the weather turned almost balmy. She took a beach chair close to the water and sipped a glass of iced tea while watching the waves. The legend of the captain and the lady finally receded from her mind.

The coast was so quiet. She would miss that part. The swells lapped their soothing rhythm and lulled her into a tranquil state. When she awoke from her sleepy reverie, the sun was setting on the horizon.

My time is almost over here. Think I will take one final walk along the shore.

She left her shoes by the chair and savored the wet sand between her toes as she meandered down the beach. The light faded and cast an ethereal glow on the landscape, and her thoughts returned to the legend of the mermaid.

Trying to be positive, she decided to think of the mermaid incident in a creative way.

What a great story for a children's book. Modified into a picture book. A mermaid's tale.

Adrift in the idea of creating the illustrations, she lost all sense of direction and landed right in front of Drake Morgan's driveway. Music poured from the open door.

Embarrassed, she turned to make a hasty retreat, but ran smack into the captain.

"Leaving without saying hello?" he smirked.

She jumped back and caught her breath. "I…I thought you might be busy, what with the music and all. Where did you come from? You weren't on the beach a minute ago."

The huge, rust colored Bullmastiff panted softly beside him, but emitted a low warning growl.

"Big dog," she stated.

"This is Magnum. An amazing companion…and watch dog. We walk every afternoon. I leave the music on. It soothes me." He leaned down to pat the dog's head. "What are you doing here?"

"You'll laugh."

"Try me, I promise I won't laugh too hard." He smiled. "Come on, I'll fix you something hot to drink."

She followed him to the cabin, reluctant, and a little fearful. She stood at the bottom of the landing and watched him enter the open door.

He turned. "Afraid you won't come back out? I told you before, I don't bite."

She shook off the odd feeling and climbed the steps.

Magnum established himself at the entrance keeping a watchful eye on her. Once inside, she blinked to adjust to the darkness. Unopened boxes littered the floor, but she spied Drake in the lighted kitchen and skirted past the disorganized array.

A heated mug of tea rested in his outstretched hand. She took it, grateful for its warmth.

"Now tell me what brings you here." He perched on a stool next to the bar and motioned for her to do the same.

Tentative, she took the one at the far end of the island. "It's silly, really. I was told this cabin was vacant, that no one had lived here in years. I thought I would see for myself. Obviously, they're wrong, that's all. Wanted to see if you were a figment of my imagination. Could be I only dreamed you fixed me breakfast." The tea acted as a distraction while she pretended to sip the hot liquid.

"It was me, alright. I'm an excellent cook if you'll remember. Look around, no one has occupied this place in years. The cabin came cheap—I needed a new place, and the price was right. I don't need much, won't be here long anyway."

Magnum's deep growl interrupted their conversation.

Drake raised his finger to his lips and motioned for her to stay put.

"Hello? Anyone home? I'm a bit afraid of your dog…" A female voice in obvious distress set the protective dog barking.

"Whoa boy, settle down." He clipped a leash onto the dog's collar. "Who are you? What do you want?"

Maren called from the kitchen, "It's Rose. Rose Clancy. She's actually the one who told me the cabin was empty."

His face grew dark. "Magnum doesn't like strangers to come too close. He doesn't like nosy people either."

"What are you doing here, Rose?" Maren brushed past the captain and his dog.

"You've gone silent after the…uh, incident the other

night. I had to come and see if you were alright. When I didn't find you at your place, I decided you might be here." She reached out a hand to Drake. "I'm Rose Clancy, as Maren said. I live about a mile down the beach."

Drake turned, went into the house with the dog, and slammed the door.

Both women continued to stare at the house. When he didn't come back out, she turned to the intrusive woman. "I should have trusted my instinct about you. You're nothing but a busybody. I had him talking and you ruined everything." She walked swiftly through the wet sand, back to her studio, leaving Rose standing alone.

The day passed pleasant and warmer. Work consumed the hours, and Maren kept to herself.

The handsome stranger didn't reappear until late that night. The air was warm, the stars were out, and the moon full and bright. Alone on the deck, a cold glass of lemonade her only companion, she sat down to enjoy the soothing sounds of the ocean rhythms. The quiet, uneventful day almost convinced her to rethink the decision to go back to the city, until she saw a figure darting in and out from behind Passion Rock. A shadow of a man illuminated by the half moon, very animated, marched back and forth.

"Is he talking to someone? It looks like Drake—he's wearing a captain's hat," she whispered.

Slow and deliberate, she descended the stairway, barefoot. The male silhouette pointed and waved his hands at an unseen companion. Her gaze held the scene, afraid it would disappear in the mist. Closer and closer, she drew…the rock glistening, electric in the midnight air. Each foot oozed deep in the wet sand, caressing and warm, and then…the sound, the plaintive, desolate cry…

The morning rays bounced off the tin star on the policeman's uniform as he questioned Rose. "Miss Clancy, you say you talked to Maren yesterday?" Officer Adams placed his pen behind one ear. "That's the last time you heard from her?"

"Yes sir—she babbled about some apparition on the water. I offered to come over and stay, but she refused…hung up the phone. Have you found anything?" Rose drew her windbreaker tighter.

"Nothing, the only clues are these water-filled footprints in the sand. They lead directly to the ocean." He pointed to the dainty prints almost obliterated by the tide.

"Footprints headed for the sea?" She followed the officer's gaze out across the water.

"Oh, I almost forgot." He pulled a beat-up captain's hat from his pocket. "Washed up on the shore. Don't make 'em like that anymore. Look familiar?"

"Why no, I've never seen it before. Have you talked to all the residents? Did they see anything?"

"A few, but no one seems to know anything. The season hasn't fully opened up quite yet," he said. "Too cold. Only a handful close enough to this cabin to do any good."

"Then how did you know Maren was missing?" Rose asked.

"Her editor from the city. Came down here to find her. Reported her disappearance to the local police." He looked closely at Rose. "Do you know more than you're telling me?"

"Look, I only glimpsed her a couple of times on the beach. She was most unfriendly. Always babbling about some

Captain Morgan. I believe she was having a breakdown of sorts. If I can be of more help, please call." Rose trudged down the beach, brushed at a stray, golden strand of wispy hair, a wry grin on her face. "Much obliged, Maren, my friend, much obliged," she whispered, as she stared out to sea.

CHAPTER FOUR

MAREN STRUGGLED TO OPEN HER EYES—TO NO AVAIL, and panic set in as the fog in her brain dissipated. *Have I been drugged?* Her head pounded. Both legs and arms felt like weights as she fought to sit up.

Finally, her heavy lids stayed open, but only total darkness engulfed her, and a rocking sensation added to her already nauseous stomach.

Where in the hell am I?

She wracked her brain for the last memory before waking up in this vault of gloom. *Where was I? On the beach?*

Bit by bit, she pieced together the sparse recollection. *I walked on the beach. But why? Oh yes, I heard the noise again and went down to Passion Rock to investigate. Touching the stone and listening to the soulful sound as it receded into the night is the last thing I remember.*

Weakness overcame her as she pushed down on the damp wooden boards beneath her and stood rather precariously. The effort took all the strength she could muster. Wobbling, but forcing her body to remain upright, she ventured a few steps. Not sure which direction to pursue, she followed her instinct with hands thrust out in front to ward off any obstacle she might encounter.

Navigation proved difficult because of the rocking motion beneath her feet. Step by step, she inched into the inky blackness trying to connect with something to give her a sense of anything familiar. Finally, she bumped into a wall and followed it hoping to discover a way out of this torture chamber.

Persistence paid off as she hit a corner and almost fell as the rocking motion pitched her forward. Fortunately, a railing caught her hand as she stumbled ahead, but she maintained her balance.

Stairs!

Hope renewed, she grasped the banister and started to climb. One foot in front of the other, the uphill effort drained any reserve energy, but eventually a door signaled the end. After fumbling in total blindness, she found the latch and pulled upward. It released.

I'm free!

She gulped hard, trying to breathe as she emerged from the dungeon-like hole, but only heavy dank air infused her lungs. Coughing ensued and she finally sputtered, "Not the fresh air I'd hoped." And again, complete darkness surrounded her. The only difference were the stars overhead. Not many, and clouds obscured what pinpoints of light she could see.

Waves crashed against the side of whatever conveyance her misfortune had landed her.

A ship of some sort, I fear.

As the vehicle rocked, she found her footing, squinting into the darkness.

"Help!" she called. "Someone please help me. I've been kidnapped. Please someone answer me."

Instead of an onslaught of footsteps to her rescue, she was met with complete silence.

No one rushed to her aid. In fact, the slap of waves against the side of the ship proved the only sound. She ventured forward inspecting the surroundings. Above her, lowered sails flapped in the slight breeze which led her to believe the ship must be an ancient type of schooner—very old and dilapidated. The realization she occupied the sailing vessel alone worried her more than anything.

"How on earth did I get here?" she spoke to the empty deck. The vessel didn't feel as if it moved forward at all. "Any ship needs an anchor. I have to find it to determine if it's just drifting or if we're sitting in one spot.

Carefully, she moved forward. Not very knowledgeable about seafaring things, she had to determine which way was fore and which aft. *I wish I had paid more attention to my father. He was the expert.* As her eyes adjusted to the darkness, she spotted what she thought was the helm. The sound of her own voice gave her comfort in an odd way. "I've gone the wrong way. The anchor has to be at the front of the boat. The ship wheel faces that way."

She headed in that direction, carefully picking her way through debris on the rotten deck. Chains, empty boxes, barrels, all sorts of wreckage. Finally, she saw the bow and checked the chain. It was let out all the way, so the anchor had been dropped.

The breeze carried her words to the nothingness of the ocean. "This is freaking me out. Anchored on an old ship with no one on board. Why? I'm stranded here. I certainly don't have the strength to pull up something that heavy. I'll either starve to death or throw myself overboard."

"Not if I have any say in it."

The deep throaty voice a slight Scottish brogue with a touch of humor, made her jump. *Drake Morgan!* She turned quickly, relieved to connect with a friend. When she faced the man, her eyes widened with surprise. Before her stood what looked like a sea captain, but his uniform didn't look at all modern. The bulky coat was tattered and worn; his hat rumpled. A sort of emblem was attached to his lapel, but she couldn't make it out. Salt and pepper, curly hair crept out from under his cap, and his gray beard had a life of its own. The dimples were there, but his half-cocked eyebrow was not. Still, this man resembled a version of Drake Morgan, but was much older.

Her breath caught. "Drake? Are you Captain Morgan?"

"Alas no, lassie. My name is Nelson."

"Where did you come from?" she spoke quickly, trying to hide the fear building in her breast.

He swept the cap from his head, the tousled curls springing every which way and bowed. "Captain Nelson, at your service. Welcome to *The Lost Opal*."

"You're not going to tell me you are Horatio Nelson are you?" she asked.

A twinkle danced in his molten eyes as he answered, "Sorry to disappoint. No, not *that* Captain Nelson. I'm just plain old Captain Henry Nelson."

"I only ask because your uniform looks like it's a hundred years old. Am I imagining all this?" She swept her hand around to encompass the ship.

He shook his head. "No, I'm afraid this is all too real. And yes, this apparel is almost two centuries old, as am I."

She gasped, "How can it be? You can't still be alive."

"I'm held in limbo, dear."

"Limbo?"

"This is all too difficult to explain on this windy old deck. Come below with me. Have a hearty cup of coffee and some warm bread. You'll feel better, then I can tell you how I came to be here."

CHAPTER FIVE

ROSE AMBLED BACK TO HER CABIN, TALKING TO THE OPEN sea. "My little chat with the policeman proved fruitful because I learned of the arrival of Maren's editor, an unexpected surprise. I hoped no one would miss her for a while. Where can this person be? Staying at Maren's place perhaps? I doubt they'll leave until some answers are found. Maybe I'll have to prod them a little."

She turned around and studied the missing woman's cabin. A single window stood open on the side of the house, and a lone figure crossed back and forth. *A woman. Should be easy enough to get rid of her.*

As she watched, a man approached the officer who still poked around the area. *Captain Drake. He seems none too pleased.*

He leaned forward, arms flailing, and pointed toward the ocean. The officer shook his head and gestured toward the cabin. Finally, the captain strode with purpose in the direction of Maren's bungalow.

Going to talk to the editor, I suppose. She followed him from a safe distance.

Drake rapped on the door.

She edged close enough so she might hear their exchange in the salty air.

He knocked again. The door opened just as he turned to go.

"Hello, my name is Drake Morgan. You must be Maren's friend." He removed his captain's cap and reached out his hand."

The woman ran a hand through her unruly shoulder-length black hair. "Why yes, I'm Telsa Stewart, her editor. She works for my company." Instead of asking him inside, she joined him on the porch. "Have you any news of her?"

"No, I hoped you had new information."

"Please, sit down." She pointed to the wicker chair. "I'd invite you in, but…"

"I understand. Maren is a private person. I gather that much about her anyway." He smiled.

"So, you don't know her well?"

"Not really. Spoke to her a couple of times. Came up behind her as I walked the beach one night. Frightened the bejesus out of her. Made her breakfast as an apology." He took off his cap and scratched his head. "She works as an illustrator in the city, but that's all I've learned so far."

Rose moved closer and decided to make her presence known. "Maren! Is that you? Oh, pardon me. I saw a woman and thought you might be her." She turned to Morgan. "Why hello, Drake. Didn't notice you there. Is there any news?" She extended her hand toward Telsa. "I'm Rose Clancy from a few cabins down."

The editor looked surprised but shook her hand. "Hello. News travels fast, I guess. When did you last see her?"

Morgan stood facing Rose, a frown on his lips. "Probably the day she tried to snoop in my business. I'd invited Maren in, and this one decided to horn in." He jabbed his finger toward Rose. "I'll leave you two to sort it all out." He scribbled on a piece of paper he retrieved from his pocket and handed it to Telsa. "This is my number. Please call me if you find out anything. She's a sweet lady." He made a quick exit and disappeared down the beach.

Telsa stared at the piece of paper.

Rose was glad he left. It made her job a bit easier. "A most unpleasant man. Never has a nice word to say."

"He seemed pleasant enough until you came along. Bad blood between you two?"

Rose laughed. "Not at all. Why would you say that?"

"Well, it's none of my business. I'm focused on finding my business associate. So, if you don't mind, unless you have pertinent news, I have phone calls to make."

"No, I don't have any news. I thought you were Maren. I won't trouble you further." Rose headed toward the steps but stopped. "Oh, don't let the strange noises at night bother you. Maren always heard weird sounds. And she saw things, too. Stay away from Passion Rock. Could be where she disappeared. Locals say it has mysterious powers, but then you don't strike me as the superstitious type."

Telsa hesitated for only a second, then disappeared inside the cabin.

Rose meandered down the sandy beach until she reached a safe distance from Maren's place. She pulled a red-orange fire opal from her pocket and held it in both hands until heat generated between her fingers. She spoke to the stone as if it was a living thing. "I speak to thee this day to bring fire down on the one called Telsa. Strike fear in her heart and compel her to go away."

The stone glowed hot, but she held tight until the stone reached a peak and slowly cooled down. She knew her spell had been received, now all she had to do was wait.

CHAPTER SIX

Maren followed Captain Henry Nelson because she didn't have a choice. She couldn't wrap her mind around his claim of being over two hundred years old, nor that he looked like Drake. *How can that be?*

They reached the hatch and descended the old wooden stairs. The chilling creak of the steps leading to the galley drove home she was indeed in a nightmare of supernatural proportions. But in the confusion and terror something else broke through to remind her of something real and comforting. The unmistakable aroma of a strong brew.

"I smell coffee. My nerves can use a cup."

"Right away, lass. Sit down and I'll serve it right up." He moved to the cooking area.

At first glimpse of the galley stove, she noticed the complexity of the contraption. "You cook on that?" The inability to comprehend where she was directed her focus elsewhere.

"I do my best. The ship is wooden, you see. So, precautions are made so fire won't go between decks. Layers of sand, sheet metal, that sort of thing. Do you want me to explain how it works or is something more pressing on your mind?" His smile was kind and the twinkle returned.

"You know I want to find out how I ended up here, but the stove caught my eye."

He started to pour the coffee into a pewter tankard.

"Wait!"

"What is it? You're not afraid I've poisoned the brew, are ya?" he asked.

"No. The cup is made of pewter, right?"

"Of course, that's what we have on board this ship." He returned the pot to the stove. "You don't expect fine China, eh lass?"

"Not at all. Surely you are aware pewter contains lead. You'll develop lead poisoning. *I'll* develop lead poisoning. Really, you can't drink from it."

A hearty laugh filled the room as Captain Nelson bent over double laughing with amusement. He sucked in a large breath and resumed his upright stance. "Oh my, girlie. I've been drinkin' my coffee out of this here mug for more than two hundred years. I've yet to observe any sign of this so-called lead poisoning. But then again, I'm in limbo. The minute I am released from this dastardly fate I'll probably fall over dead from one disease or other."

She wrinkled her nose at the lame attempt at humor. "Suppose you tell me more about this limbo thing. Meanwhile, I'll pass on the coffee, although the aroma is wonderful."

He scratched his beard. "Tell ya what. I have a small ceramic cup I use for measurin'. Would you be compelled to drink out of that? I'd be horrified if you couldn't enjoy the comfort of a stout cup of coffee."

"Oh yes. Do you have any sugar or cream?"

His eyes narrowed. "I only have a wee bit of sugar and none at all of the cream. Us sailors drink our coffee black. Puts hair on your chest."

Heat seared her cheeks. "Er, black is fine. And I don't want to use your sugar."

"Ah, but I'm the wily one." He laughed. "I'm only joshin' ya again. I've no use for sugar here. You can have all you want. But

I wasn't lying about the cream. Never has been any of that on this old sea rover."

He poured the coffee, stirred in a bit of sugar, then handed it to her.

She breathed in the strong aroma, then took a sip. "Oh, it's wonderful, just perfect. Thank you."

He swept off his cap and gave a dramatic bow. "At your service, miss. Been a while since I've had any company to speak of. I hardly remember how to behave." He grabbed a plate of sliced bread, a dollop of butter, sat down across from her, and took a long swig from his tankard. "Now, let's talk."

"Yes, thank you." She buttered the bread and took a small bite. "So good. Did you bake this? How in the world do you have fresh butter?"

"Of course I baked it. Do you see anyone else on this ship? As far as the butter goes, we're in limbo here. Everything is replenished every day. Don't ask me how. It just is. Do you want to hear more, or shall we wait until you've had your fill?"

She swiped her hand across her mouth to rid herself of the crumbs and shook her head. "I want you to tell everything. I'm a bit hungry is all. Please go on."

He leaned forward. "Since you're here on this ship I'm guessin' you've met the Kaaiman."

"Kaaiman? Why no, I'm not sure what you're talking about."

"Aye, you probably heard it by the name mermaid. She's a sea wraith and has only evil in mind. She seeks revenge and won't rest until she secures a human body so she can live permanently on land."

She almost dropped the cup but managed to hang on. "A mermaid? You mean they're real? Why, I've seen an apparition. At Passion Rock. But what has that got to do with me?"

He nodded. "You've encountered her, aye?"

"Well, yes and no. I heard strange cries, but never actually saw anything. Every time I edged close to the vision, it moved away and disappeared into the water."

He nodded. "Since you're here, I'm guessing she's chosen you as her replacement."

He took another swig from his cup. "Oh, you had to have a conversation. She secures her victims in that manner. Casts a spell. That's how you landed on this ship. She carries a small red-orange opal. Probably conceals the thing in her clothing. But when you're near enough, she grasps it and casts the spell. Does the name Lillith mean anything to you?"

She thought a moment. "No, only in mythology. Wasn't she supposed to be Adam's first wife, you know, of the bible? The myth suggests she was created the same time as Adam, but wouldn't be subservient to him, so God cast her out. That's when he created Eve from Adam's rib. I've always considered it a fable. But I've never met anyone named Lillith."

He stood to pour more coffee and leaned over to refill her cup, as well. "Well then, she also goes by the name Rose, symbolizing perfection. The only association she has to a rose is the thorny stems. She uses the name to lure the men into her web of lies. When one thinks of a rose, they mostly think of the sweet fragrance and the luscious color."

She jerked up so fast the cup tumbled over. The hot liquid spread across the wooden table and dripped down the edge, spilling over on her clothes. "Oh, I'm sorry." She tried to brush the wetness from her jeans.

Captain Nelson clucked his tongue and reached for a cloth. "Ah, I've hit a nerve." He wiped the liquid from the table. "So, you *do* know a woman named Rose?"

"Yes, Rose Clancy. I've only just met her. However, I did have a bad feeling about her from the beginning."

Nelson poured her another cup and scooted the sugar closer to her. "Ah yes, that would be her, right enough."

"I'm still confused. What reason does she have to do this to me? She did try to spook me with the story of the mermaid thing. But again, I ask. Why me?"

He lowered his chin to his hand, thumped his finger against his beard, and asked, "Was there a captain involved anywhere in your acquaintance on the beach?"

"Why yes, a Captain Drake Morgan. Why?"

He slapped his knee. "Ah, the one you mistook me for. That's it. You must have gotten in her way of the pursuit of the captain. She had to eliminate you. Time is of the essence for her. From the day she meets him, she has thirty days in which to lure him under her spell. After that, she loses the power to attract him, and she is regulated back to the sea. You simply got in her way."

"But, I have no interest in him. Curiosity, maybe, but that's all." She stood again, voice shaking, "I've got to leave this boat. I have a life back there. My deadline is coming up soon and I can't miss it!"

He shook his head. "Sorry, miss, but there's no way off this vessel until the day Lillith fails to win the heart of a captain."

Her eyes widened. "You mean she's done this to others?"

He nodded with a frown. "Many others. A different woman each year. And she hasn't failed yet. I'm afraid you're stuck with me."

She glanced around. "If she succeeded then others must be aboard this ship. Where are they?"

He hesitated. "Come with me, little one." He rose and trudged up the stairs.

When they got to the deck, he leaned against the side. "Out there." He pointed across the water.

She followed where he indicated. "I don't understand. What do you mean, out there?"

"They jumped into the sea and died there."

Shivers ran up and down her spine and she began to shake. "Why did they jump?"

"Time runs long aboard a marooned ship, dearie. They couldn't take the endless days and lonely nights. Rather die than live an existence of never-ending doom. You see once you leave the ship without the protection of the Kaaiman, you die. That is why I've lived so long. I refuse to leave until I find a way out."

She stared at the waves lapping against the side of the ship—dark, murky water, with no moonlight to lift complete blackness from the night. "Those women, drowned…doomed." She whirled on him. "Is that what is going to happen to me? I'll simply go mad? There's no recourse?"

He placed his hands on her shoulders. "Might be a way, but in all these years, I've not found the bugger. Neither did the others. I've scoured every inch of this old tub. It's not here."

"What? What's not here?"

"Let's go back down to the galley. The story is better coming in a bit of light, rather than this dank darkness."

She followed him, a spark of hope beating in her breast.

Surely I can find what he seeks and free us both.

CHAPTER SEVEN

MAGNUM WHINED FROM INSIDE THE CABIN AS DRAKE Morgan hurried to unlock the door. "Sorry old boy, but it wouldn't do for me to take you with me this time. I had to talk with the police officer without any interference from you."

The dog jumped onto his master, both powerful paws on Drake's shoulders, as he welcomed him home, licking his face, his body contorting as his tail wagged back and forth.

"I know, I know. I hated to lock you up, but it couldn't be helped." He lifted the huge paws off of him and leaned down to scruff the neck of his deep-chested companion. "Come to the kitchen, I have your favorite treat."

The faithful dog followed close to his master's side, almost tripping him.

"Now, now, I'm back and I'm not going to leave you again, so give me some room." Drake laughed at his dog. The large canine was only seven months old when he acquired him. They'd bonded instantly. Now three years old, the puppy phase was waning, except the big galoot suffered from separation anxiety. Training had been a breeze, however, and he contributed that to the bonding.

He opened a plastic container and tossed the bacon tidbit to Magnum who scooped it up and swallowed it whole. "I wish you wouldn't do that. It's harder for you to digest, but then, who am I kidding? You're gonna do what you're gonna do, aren't you?"

Drake made coffee before he left to talk to the officer and the pot was still warm. He poured a cup and sat down at the small table in the breakfast nook.

Magnum nudged Morgan's leg aside and curled up on his bed at his master's feet, tail beating a steady rhythm against the floor. The dog bed was a jumbo size, but he still hung over the edges.

He spoke aloud while scratching the dog's ear. "What do you think has become of Maren? I wasn't alarmed at first because she made it known she needs privacy, but no one has seen or heard from her. And those footprints in the sand leading to the water. Not sure what to make of that."

The eager canine answered with a renewed wagging of his tail.

"Wonder if I can aid in the search."

As he contemplated this thought, a knock provoked a growl from Magnum.

"Hold on, boy. It might be news of Maren." He ordered the dog to stay and went to the door.

"Rose? What are you doing here? I'm busy." Annoyance permeated his speech.

"Why, Captain. Is that any way to greet a concerned citizen? I've come to suggest a meeting of the minds. If we work together, we might unravel Maren's sudden disappearance. She was prone to walking the beach toward your cabin but might have wandered farther down."

He purposely didn't open the screen that separated them. "That wouldn't account for the prints leading to the sea by Passion Rock, and there weren't any headed toward my place. I propose we let the police do their jobs."

"Of course, I agree, but we're neighbors worried about a

friend. Two heads are better than one. Why you sound as if you don't care what happens to her. Sorry to have bothered you." She turned and walked halfway down the steps.

He sighed deeply. "Alright, alright. I wouldn't want her to think I wasn't concerned when she does turn up." The screen door swung open. "Come in and have a cup of coffee. We might uncover something the police haven't thought of."

She did a slow pivot, a smile lighting her face. "I'm so pleased you reconsidered. I'd love some."

He led her into the kitchen, pointed to a bar chair next to the island, and grabbed another cup from the cupboard. "How do you like yours? Sugar, cream?"

"Oh, black for me. I like to keep it simple."

He nodded, poured hers, and refilled his. "Now, what's your timeline? When is the last time you talked to her?"

He noticed the blush stain her cheeks, but she answered in a controlled manner. "It was the afternoon you and she were inside your cabin. I happened along, saw the door open, and called out. I was afraid of your dog if you remember. You said something rude, went back into the house, and slammed the door. Maren accused me of meddling and left in a huff, leaving me standing there. I haven't seen her since. What about you?"

His mood didn't improve as he listened. He remembered his dislike of Rose and her nosy ways. The assessment still stood. "I'm afraid that's the last time I saw her, as well. I'd say she went back to the city, but we agree that isn't what happened because her editor is here looking for her."

"I have a couple of friends that were at the clam bake a few days ago. Maybe one of them has seen her. There's one in particular, Josh. He's sweet on her. Could be she ended up with him."

Drake stood, hoping this little interview was over. "That's reasonable. I suppose the police are asking around town. I need some groceries. I'll see if the locals know anything."

Rose slipped off the bar chair and sidled up close beside him. She touched his arm. "Sounds like a plan. Listen, why don't you come to my place for dinner this evening. We can share what we've learned."

He shook his head. *That's the last thing I want to do.* "Thanks, but I'll take a raincheck. I've plans tonight."

Magnum placed himself next to his master and growled.

"Your dog is certainly intimidating. He scares me. I hope you have good control of him." She put her cup down and walked toward the door. "I wish you'd reconsider about dinner. I'll let you know what Josh and his friends say. Thanks for the coffee."

Drake followed her with Magnum on his heels. "Same here. Goodbye, Rose."

He kept eyes on her as she headed toward her cabin. At one point, she turned, both hands in her pockets, and watched him, but whirled quickly and marched away.

Slowly, he closed the door. "That one is a piece of work. Instinct tells me to stay as far away as possible. But I was rude. Can't help myself when it comes to her. She's so obvious. Still, not an excuse to be so brusque. I'm sure she's harmless."

Rose walked quickly until she was a fair distance away from Drake's cabin. She turned, clutched the opal, and cast the spell. "Soften Captain Morgan's heart and compel him to be receptive to my advances." The heat of the stone reassured her.

The captain watches me from his doorway. She smiled. *The gem will do its work.*

Once inside her cabin, she set about preparations for dinner, confident he would change his mind. To the empty room, she said, "Telsa will go back to the city, the captain will be mine, and Maren will be forgotten."

She fingered the mermaid shaped amulet resting against her heart, a constant reminder of the fate awaiting her should she fail to win the captain's affections. Within the intricate design, inlaid with blue silver-fire opals encircled by diamonds, her tormented soul lay trapped inside.

She must find a replacement and a captain to love her or face another year of a watery existence until she was released once again.

Each year was the same. A new search, a new love for over two hundred years. The first was Captain Nelson and she was convinced he loved her, but it was a lie. His transgression damned him to *The Lost Opal,* the ship he cared about more than her, and will be his home for eternity. In return she must honor the code of the spell and renew her freedom every year.

He'll stay there forever if I have anything to say about it.

Drake clipped the leash to Magnum's collar and proceeded down the stairs to fulfil his promise to Rose. Someone in town may have a simple solution to Maren's sudden exit. The thought crossed his mind that she and her editor passed each other in transit. Maren might have wanted to surprise Ms. Stewart and returned to the city unannounced. *Happens all the time in the movies.*

There were no airports close to the beach, so he tried the bus station. No one by that name or description bought a ticket to anywhere. *Who am I kidding? Her SUV was still there beside the cabin. She would have driven it home, not taken the bus. The more I think about it, the more troublesome it becomes. I only hope Rose has better luck with Josh and the other friends.*

Hunger reminded him it was about lunch time, so he chose a little outdoor bistro. It was crowded, but he found a table, ordered

Magnum to lie down, and waited for the waiter to come by. The air was buzzing about Maren's mysterious disappearance.

News sure travels fast. But I suppose the police have already made the rounds fueling the speculation. He listened intently, hoping to pick up a tidbit that might lead to an answer, but none came. Eventually, the waiter came to take his order, but his appetite had waned. He ordered a beer and sipped on it listening for any new information.

The beer was gone and so was his patience. He clucked his tongue to Magnum, and they left via the garden gate.

On the slow walk home, he had to pass by Rose's cabin. Hoping to avoid her, he quickened his pace, but was too late.

She waved him down. "Captain! I can't wait to hear what you've found out. Any luck, at all?"

He kept walking but slowed to address her question. "None. No one has seen her. No bus ticket, nothing."

She reached out a hand. "Please, won't you come in for a moment? I'd like to share with you what I've found. I spoke to Josh and the others."

He stopped, aware of his rudeness before. "Look, Magnum needs to be fed and I need my lunch, as well. Why don't you tell me right here? Or better yet, share it with the police."

Her face fell. She slipped her outstretched hand into the pocket of her beachcomber skirt to clutch the amulet. "I have dogfood. I can fix you a sandwich. Won't you reconsider?"

"Magnum needs a certain blend, and I wouldn't want to trouble you." He started back down the beach, but guilt seized him. He turned back to her. "Tell you what. How about I come for dinner this evening? You can tell me all about it then. I really need to feed the dog. He's cantankerous enough, wouldn't want to add to his already questionable behavior." He felt the strange beginnings of a smile on his face. *What am I saying? I don't want to have dinner with her.*

The 'poor me' look left her face immediately. "Oh, that's wonderful. Come a bit early for a drink. We can discuss the disappearance before dinner."

He fought the strange tenderness for her, shook himself, nodded, and walked on.

"Five-thirty then. Don't be late," she called.

⇒✺⇐

Rose opened the door at precisely the appointed hour when Drake Morgan knocked. "Good evening. I'm pleased you're so punctual." She looked around the captain's feet. "You didn't bring Magnum?"

"No, he's asleep in his bed. It was a perfect time to slip out."

"Please come in," she said.

She showed him where to sit." I'll be right back with the drinks."

In the kitchen, she placed two high ball glasses on a serving tray and filled a pitcher with one third vodka, one fourth peach schnapps, and a cup of grapefruit juice. She mixed it well and poured. The finishing touch was verbena, the drug of enchantment. Sprinkled generously on top, the herb would be the first thing the intended target would intake, rendering them hopelessly in love. She was careful not to put too much or too little. One would make them impotent, the other would make them sleep. The measurement had to be precise.

She carefully carried the tray into the living room and offered him a glass.

"What's this?" he asked.

"A specialty of mine. I hope you like vodka. Please give it a try," she coaxed.

He took the cocktail and passed it beneath his nose. "Smells wonderful. I'm usually a beer or whiskey guy, but I'll give it a try."

She lifted hers from the tray and studied him closely as he took a tentative sip.

"Mmm. Tastes great, very refreshing." After another swig, he asked. "What's for dinner? And what is the news you want to give me?"

"Kabobs. I wanted to keep it simple. I hope you'll enjoy them." She continued to watch him as he finished the beverage. "As far as any news, I'm afraid I struck out. What about you?"

A strange look washed over his face. One she hadn't seen before. The sharpness of his unpleasantness melted away, a smile dressed his lips, and his eyes twinkled.

"Captain? Did you hear what I said? Are you quite alright? You're a little flushed."

Drake sat up a bit straighter. "My God, I've never noticed before how beautiful you are."

Her lips curved into a seductive smile as she moved closer to him.

Exactly the reaction I wanted you to have, my dear Captain Morgan.

CHAPTER EIGHT

MAREN DRUMMED HER NAILS ON THE TABLE AS CAPTAIN Nelson refilled the coffee cups, pulled out a few potatoes, and began to peel. "I'm not hungry. Please, sit and tell me what this object is you need to find?"

He turned from the preparations; the paring knife clutched in his hand. "Alas, my friend, you cannot do a proper search without sustenance. We've plenty of time, you see. Without the talisman you aren't going anywhere for at least thirty days. One of the few things I enjoy in my captivity is eating a hearty meal."

Thirty days? I'm stuck on this ship for that long? There **has** *to be something I can do.*

"You talk of a talisman, what exactly is that?" she asked.

He finished the peeling and pulled an onion to the chopping board. "No one knows for sure. It could be anything." He reached for the salt and pepper and seasoned the meat. "An object like a ring, a brooch, a necklace, or something entirely different. An inscription is somewhere inside or on the back that sets the doomed one free if said aloud while holding the object."

"And you've searched the entire ship?"

"More than once, dearie. I've had more than two hundred years to find it. Rose told me I'd fail because I love no one but myself and *The Lost Opal*. Said that love of the ship will blind me because I can't see past my own shortcomings." He paused and looked up as if in thought. "Maybe she was right."

"What about the other women, did they look?"

"Oh yes, tore the ship apart. Their disappointment was so deep they couldn't face a life on this ship. They…well, I don't have to repeat what happened." Satisfied with the seasoning, he placed the roast, potatoes, and onion in a shallow pan, poured broth on top, and shut the oven door with a slam. "Now, in about an hour we'll feast!"

"You haven't shown me where I'll sleep, Captain. Could we do that now? I'd like to rest before we eat."

"Certainly, lass. Your quarters are this way. Follow me." He led her up the stairs.

She'd read enough books and seen enough pirate movies to ascertain where the captain's rooms were located, and he led her straight there.

"Here we are." He opened the door and stepped aside.

The room gleamed and a light scent of lemon wafted through the air. She ran her hand over the banister as she walked down the short stairway. No dust, a perfectly made bed, and a desk with a map laid out told the story of a very meticulous captain.

"It's beautiful," she whispered. "But I can't take your cabin. You're the captain of this ship."

"Ah, dearie. This is my in-port quarters. I never use them. I have out-port quarters near the bridge. I'd rather sleep there since I don't have a crew. So, you'll have all the amenities and privacy."

In awe, she walked around the spacious accommodations. A bay window allowed light inside and gave a view of the ocean. Right now, it was dark, no moon, but she could see a sprinkling of stars. Maybe the morning will set my heart at ease.

The captain moved toward the door. "I'll leave you to get adjusted to your new accommodations. I'll call you when the meal is ready. Get some rest."

The door closed softly behind him.

Tired, but curious, she walked around the cabin, opening doors, the closet, and desk drawers. "It's unlikely I'd find this amulet in such obvious places, but I have to start somewhere."

Of course, the search yielded nothing, not even a clue. She sat on the bed and looked around the room, inspecting the ceiling, the floor, and the walls.

She tapped her index finger on her chin and said, "If I were a mermaid, where would I hide an amulet?"

In her entire life, she never thought she'd ever utter words like that. She laughed and pondered the situation again.

Nothing came to her. *Well, maybe more clues will emerge as I talk to the captain.*

The bed was surprisingly comfortable as she eased back, placing her head on the pillow. *Captain said about an hour. I can close my eyes for a bit.*

Sleep overtook her almost instantly. Disjointed dreams swirled in her weary mind, making restorative rest impossible. Dark churning water, claustrophobic blackness smothered her, the rocking motion brought on nausea to the point of physical heaving. Sweating broke out while she tossed and turned. A dark shadow pointed a bony finger toward her as she faded away into darkness, losing her soul, while the high cackle of the apparition sounded all around her.

She let out a piercing scream and was immediately comforted by a strong, friendly hand on her shoulder.

She bolted upright. "Captain? What? Where am I?"

"You were having a nightmare, lassie. I heard moaning, then a scream. I decided to wake you. Don't worry, you're safe for now. You're damp from sweat. It must have been a bad dream, for sure. Sit still for a moment, I'll be right back."

A frantic glance around the room brought back the memory

of her situation. Apprehension gripped her as she waited for his return.

"Here we are. Now just let me tend to you." He placed a damp cloth to her forehead and held it there. In his other hand he carried a cup of a strong-smelling liquid. "Drink this."

Her nose wrinkled at the pungent odor. "What is it?"

"It's a tea. Especially for stomach issues. I saw you heaving before I woke you. Mint and a little beer. Smells funny but works wonders. Down the hatch now." He held it to her lips.

She blinked a couple of times, then stopped. "I can't."

"Hold your nose and swallow in one gulp. You'll feel better in no time."

She pinched her nose and did as she was told. In one gulp she had the potion down.

The effect was instant. The nausea left, her head cleared, and clouds of the nightmare disappeared.

"I don't believe beer and mint is all that's in this. Care to tell me the rest of the ingredients?"

A loud belly laugh was his answer. "Come, Maren. Dinner is almost ready. You need a good meal to right your ship."

She followed him out of the cabin and to the galley. "It smells wonderful. I'm actually hungry now."

"I thought you would be. Will you pour the coffee while I dish up the meal?"

They arranged the meal on the table in complete affability and sat down to eat.

For the first few minutes, they ate in silence, Maren hardly able to stop shoveling the roast and potatoes into her mouth.

"I've never tasted such a wonderful roast. Pardon my lack of manners. I'm starved. What is your secret?"

"Ah, what kind of a cook would I be if I gave out my secrets? Why there might be a mutiny!" His belly jiggled with laughter again.

She smiled. "Oh, I'll get it from you in time. Never you fear. More coffee?"

He nodded.

The brew was rich and robust, the aroma much needed therapy for her unsettling circumstances.

She leaned back in her chair, satisfied. "I need to know more about this amulet, Captain. Suppose you tell me a little more, so I know what to look for."

He pushed his cap back, away from his brow and scratched his forehead. "Not anymore to tell, really. I don't know what the thing looks like, or I'd have found it by now. All I know is it's something unusual. Every blame thing on this ship looks like it belongs here. I've been stumped for a very long time."

"Okay, you said on the ship. What about the outside? Have you looked there?"

"I've searched around the outer sides of this old vessel, but nothing stands out. We're in the middle of a deep ocean. I can hardly go over the side and look underneath."

She remained silent as her mind ran over the possibilities of a location outside of the ship. Nothing came to her. "What about the masts? Have you looked up there? The crow's nest for instance?"

"I've sure enough looked up there. Scared the bejesus out of me. It's not easy to climb up there without someone spottin' ya in case of a fall. Most of the time I'm alone here until Rose sends another unfortunate lassie to her doom."

His statement made her shiver, but she said nothing.

"Come, let's stroll around the deck. The stars are out. It's a pleasant diversion. We'll clean up later," he suggested.

Arm in arm, they walked around the deck.

He's right, it's a pleasant diversion. How can he stay so positive after so many years of captivity? Is he just resigned to his fate?

CHAPTER NINE

Rose sat close beside Morgan on the divan, brazenly slid her hand over his knee, and gave him her most seductive smile. "Thank you for the compliment, Drake. May I call you Drake? Captain Morgan seems so formal. After all, we are becoming friends, aren't we?"

He looked down at her hand and cut his eyes toward her. "Why yes, I prefer it." His free hand cupped over hers while he took another drink of the cocktail. "This is so tasty. May I have another?"

She leaned close and plucked the glass from his hand, satisfied of the potion's viability at his slurred words. "Oh, I think not. This particular mix carries a powerful after-punch. I wouldn't want you to lose your faculties before you had something in your stomach." She reached for his hand. "Come, let's eat our dinner."

"Anything you say beautiful woman." He accepted the offer and followed her to the kitchen.

This spell is working better than I could have imagined. He's putty in my hands.

He ate with gusto, his eyes ravaging every feature of her body with open desire.

At first, she welcomed the once-over, almost reveled in it. But when he rested his gaze on her ample cleavage in blatant fashion, the perusal became uncomfortable even for her. *Did I put too much verbena in the drink?*

"Captain, let's stick to business. What did you find out?"

"About what?" He continued to stare at her bust.

His heated ogling made her place a hand across her chest. "Why Drake, did you forget about Maren? We're supposed to be working together to find out what happened to her. You went to town earlier. Did you find out anything?"

Slowly, he changed his scrutiny of her bosom to her face. "Who? Maren? Oh, yes, I didn't find out anything. Everyone is puzzled at her disappearance." He licked his lips. "What shade of lipstick are you wearing?" He slid his hand across the table and covered hers. "I'd like to kiss it right off your mouth."

Oh dear, this will never do. He's supposed to fall in love, not act like a rutting bull. Did I get the ingredients wrong? "Captain Morgan," she said sharply. "If you can't behave, then I have no choice but to end this little soiree. Come back tomorrow when you sober up." She stood and went to the door.

He followed her, swaying like a land lubber on a bobbing ship. "Oh now, Rose, we're only now getting to know each other. Remember you are the one who invited me. Your flirting is rather obvious. So, are you simply a tease?" He moved dangerously close to her yearning mouth.

His spicy cologne weakened her resolve to throw him out and she almost relented.

He leaned closer. "Do you really want me to go? I'm not sure I can make it home. Can't I stay here tonight? I promise I'll be good, darlin.' Real good."

She flung open the door and pointed to the beach. "You're just like the rest. Only one thing on your mind. Now leave."

He gave her a pouty look and cocked his brow. "Why my dear, I thought you wanted this. I must say I'm wounded to the core. I aim to please, though, so I'll go…for now. But you should lock your doors because I'm not sure I can wait until tomorrow."

"Go!"

He pushed his cap back and the ebony curls spilled forward. "Women. Never know what they want."

She closed the door and leaned against it, her pulse racing. "Lord knows I'd like nothing better than to bed him, but it can't be for physical reasons. I must have his heart and his soul."

The book of spells lay on her night table, and she hurried to retrieve it. Flipping through the pages, she came upon the concoction she'd given to Drake. "Damn! I didn't see the warning at the bottom." Under the list of ingredients, in letters almost too small to read, 'Not meant for love potion, only for physical attraction.' "That's what I get for trying something new."

Over the years Rose tried many avenues to secure the passion she so desperately wanted. Spells, concoctions, trickery, anything to achieve the love that would set her free. Sometimes they worked, but mostly the sentiment was fleeting and would end with her doomed to the ocean once again.

"Captain Nelson put all of this in motion. A selfish man who played with my heart and is suffering the consequences… and *will* until the spell is unlocked."

Passion Rock is the portal of the mermaids. There I will summon the Goddess of the Sea to help me.

Drake stumbled down the beach toward his cabin, suppressing a giggle, while keeping the façade going. He maintained his ruse until he reached his doorstep and collapsed in laughter once inside. Malcom knocked him down in his excitement. He licked his face until force was necessary to remove his paws from his shoulders. Once the dog was controlled, he climbed to his feet and allowed himself a first-rate belly laugh. "Malcom, you should have seen her. I had her going for sure. Why she thought I'd take advantage of her right then and there. Stupid woman. I've seen women like her by the dozens. She forgets I'm a sailor and can hold my liquor. That little cocktail of hers had no effect on me whatsoever, but there was a funny buzz to it. It had more than vodka in it. Even drunk I'm not sure I'd be that bold." He shrugged. "Oh well, Rose, you'll need to try harder than that to lure me to bed."

The dog wagged his tail so hard Drake thought it would fall off. "You understand, don't you boy? Malcolm, that woman has something up her sleeve and I'm going to find out what."

CHAPTER TEN

MAREN SETTLED INTO BED STILL MULLING OVER CAPTAIN Nelson's description of the amulet. 'An inscription is somewhere inside or on the back that sets the doomed one free if said aloud while holding the object.'

"An inscription," she whispered into the darkened room.

Her thoughts drifted back to that night on the beach when Rose shared a chant.

'Beware the siren's song of the sea,
Lest you're drawn like moth to flame.
For one mistake will require the key
To retrieve your soul from whence it came'

She couldn't recall the exact words, only that it chilled her to the bone. Particularly the word 'key.' "Instead of looking for the amulet itself, maybe we should be searching for a key of sorts."

Fragments came to her as she tried to remember the second verse.

Something about a hidden clue, pieces of eight and a reveal.

"Dang," she shouted. "I should have paid more attention. Truth is, those words unsettled me so much, I pushed them from my mind. If I tell the captain what I remember, he might make some sense of it." She yawned as drowsiness claimed her and she settled lower into the downy pillow. "It'll keep 'til morning."

Sleep came easily although fraught with fractured

nightmares. The high-pitched sound of a mermaid's song, a clam bake attended by floating entities chanting in sing-song fashion. Even Captain Henry infiltrated the nightmarish delusions, pointing to the plank and insisting she fling herself into the ocean. She awoke in a sweat. The dreams unnerved her to the point she didn't want to go back to sleep. Instead, she sat up, pulled on a wrap, and slid her feet into the cozy mules the captain provided her. She marveled at the conveniences he was able to produce; a set of striped pajamas (although obviously for the male gender), a cocoa brown cotton robe (again made for a man), a pair of slightly too large matching slippers. Not one to complain, however, she wrapped the warm garment tighter around her and padded to the desk, struck a match to light the lantern, and sat down.

The black swivel chair was surprisingly comfortable, a Victorian tufted relic she guessed. She spun around slowly taking in the whole room until she was drawn to the bay type window. The stars glittered in the moonless sky, and a dire pang of homesickness enveloped her. *That night at the beach, they twinkled exactly like this. I'd give anything to hear Josh's voice again, trying to persuade me to go out with him. A stupid wish, for sure, but one that brings back the need for something silly in order to feel normal.*

Morgan's handsome face, the raised brow, the abundance of black curls spilling from under his cap entered her thoughts, as well. *I'd let him cook breakfast for me every morning if I could just get back home.*

She remembered when she first heard Captain Henry's voice and thought he was Drake. *The resemblance is uncanny. They even sound alike. The age difference aside, they are dead ringers. How is that possible? Can they be relatives somehow, even if their names don't match? I'm going to press the captain at breakfast about this oddity.*

The stars continued to wink at her. She tore her gaze from the heavens, rose from the chair, and made a turn around the room, hoping for a clue to get her out of this crazy situation.

He is certainly well-read judging by the number of books in his library.

One whole wall housed extensive reading material. She'd scanned the collection when she first arrived in this room but didn't look closely. *Now is as good a time as any to explore them in a more meticulous way.*

The top shelves touched the ceiling, and she made use of the small stool in front of the first row. Even with the added height, she barely reached the highest ledge. The majority of volumes were maritime related and spanned the first four rows. Instructions on masts and sails, on navigation devices, basic sailing practices, maps of different regions, all written in the seventeen hundreds or before. As she scaled down, the subjects turned to lighter reading. Robinson Crusoe, Gulliver's Travels, the Rime of the Ancient Mariner. The sea a central theme in all texts. *I'm amazed he is so knowledgeable.*

She lovingly admired the leather-bound books, worn from use, touching them with care. *These are priceless. I wish I could take them back with me when I return. I wonder…might there be a clue hidden in these old volumes?*

She continued assessing every row, carefully studying each book. The next to the last shelf resembled diaries or captain's logs and she all but dismissed them until one in particular caught her eye. The title simply read *Grimoire*.

Hmm, looks like French…and sounds French if I have my pronunciation correct. I don't recall seeing this word before in my French classes and have no idea what it means. The sound echoed as she spoke it outloud. "grim-WAHR, or at least I think that is the way they would pronounce it."

She lifted it from the shelf. The cover was well worn, the pages well used. She opened the first page and stared at the familiar words. *Livre de sorts.* "Book of Spells," she whispered. "Why does Captain Henry have this?"

The entire text was written in French, and she could translate much of it. *This is going to take some study, but a solution might be in here somewhere.*

Instead of returning the book to its place, she carried it with her. The bed was cold, and it took a few minutes to warm. She struggled through a couple of pages before sleep insisted on making an entrance, the book falling upon her chest, a companion to her dreamless slumber.

⁂

Captain Henry paced the top deck unable to rest. He'd stopped in front of Maren's door but noticed a light streaming under the threshold. Compelled to intrude to see if all was well, he resisted the idea and continued pacing.

I'm not surprised she can't sleep. Happens to all the women who come aboard this ship, but somehow, Maren is different. I can't place where I've seen her before because there is a familiarity about her. Wherever it is, my time here has erased that memory.

A glimmer of anticipation flickered in him as he thought of her. *She is levelheaded and forthright. Can she find the clue needed to release this insidious circumstance I've suffered for so long?* He sighed. *If anyone can, it's Maren, but I dare not hope too much. Many have tried. All have failed.*

Once more he hesitated in front of her quarters and debated whether to knock. He raised his hand to the door but stopped when darkness replaced the streaming light. *She's gone to bed. I won't disturb her now.*

He lowered his hand and resumed pacing. *I've been a selfish oaf all these years. All Rose wanted was someone to love her.*

He couldn't give her what she craved. Now one more woman is doomed to share his fate. *If I could only find the amulet so Maren might be set free, I'll accept my destiny.*

He remembered the first time he saw Rose. She was beautiful and captured his interest immediately. The flirtation grew into something more intense until his ability to resist her charms evaporated. He bed her, knowing full well he'd never commit to the lifestyle she wanted. His heart lay out there, on the open water, sailing the world, tasting the fruits of numerous lands and dozens of women, leaving a string of broken hearts. Oh, he promised many things to them. To Rose, his assurance he would return was a step he never took before and would prove his undoing. Alas, she faded from his mind once he was aboard *The Lost Opal*, churning through the turbulent waters, giving rise to his sense of adventure and the freedoms that gave him purpose. He never thought of her again until the day she appeared in the calm water near a tropical island. She feigned drowning and begged him to save her. She looked familiar, but he never put the pieces to that puzzle together until his men lowered a lifeboat. When they pulled her aboard, they were stunned. A mermaid. A real-life mermaid. As she emerged her tail disappeared, and she became a whole woman. It was then he recalled the beauty he'd trifled with so many years before. Once on the ship, she faced him and directed her full wrath toward him with a curse.

He struggled to remember the words, but they escaped him. As soon as the spell was issued, she dove back into the water and returned to her former self, a mermaid once more. She swam away issuing the same anathema. He watched in disbelief as her long tail flipped once before she disappeared into the ocean.

What happened next was seared into his memory. The ship began to spin, faster and faster, caught up in a vortex like a tornado. When it stopped, he was alone, everyone was gone, and he drifted upon the sea, moored in the middle of nowhere. He tried to pull anchor, but to no avail. It would not budge. And now, over two hundred years later, nothing had changed. No ship passed by to rescue him, land was completely out of sight, and he was left to contemplate his folly.

Until Maren came he remained steadfast in the belief he did nothing wrong that warranted this punishment. But she somehow softened his crusty stance, and he saw the wickedness he'd bestowed on so many women. It was nothing she said exactly, but more her demeanor of honor, her concern for him, the determination to find a solution. The other's spent their time bellowing about their fate, concerned only with themselves, demanding he do something.

Maren was different, in that she showed genuine regard for his welfare. The pewter cup which would give him lead poisoning stood out. They both knew if this spell were solved his death would be immediate, but she insisted he not drink from the contaminated vessel anyway.

Yes, she is different. Maybe she can solve this hellish situation and release us both from this bondage.

CHAPTER ELEVEN

Drake Morgan fell asleep in the lone recliner in the living room, a glass of Tennessee Whisky in his hand. He was startled awake as the dog's wet nose nudged his hand.

Malcolm whined.

"Oh sorry, boy. Guess the whiskey was my ticket to dreamland. Need to go out, huh?" He pulled upright and gingerly extracted himself from the chair, his head pounding from a hangover. "Come on, let's go."

As he opened the front door, the darkness of night surprised him. He glanced at the only clock in the house. The digital display on the stove read one a.m.

"Wow, did I sleep that long, Malcolm? I bet you really have to go, right boy?"

The dog's nose pressed against the door, and as it opened, he bolted out in search of a place to relieve himself.

Drake grabbed his pipe and tobacco and settled into a porch chair to wait on his best friend. "Way to go, Captain. Poor dog. He sure was patient. I need to be more responsible or I'll…" An eerie iridescent light drew his attention away from his only companion. It came from Passion Rock. A humming noise added to the unusual spectral. "What in tarnation is that?"

Malcolm bounded up on the porch wagging his tail and

panting happily. His demeanor changed abruptly, however, as he turned toward the edifice and growled, his mane standing on end.

Drake patted his head and slowly wrapped his fingers around his collar. "Sit, boy."

The dog obeyed but kept a rumble going deep in his chest.

"Yeah, I should check this out, but you need to go in the cabin until I determine what's up over there." He stood with his grip still on the collar and managed to push Malcolm inside without incident.

When he turned back to the light it had grown brighter, and the humming grew in intensity. A voice pierced through the sound and a sing-song incantation rose above all else.

He couldn't make out the words nor did he recognize the voice.

Malcolm whined from behind the door, but if he let him out, he'd just spook whatever it was, and he didn't want that. Maren had mentioned a chant given by Rose on the day of the clambake. *Can it be her?* He'd love nothing more than to catch her in some nefarious act he could hold over her head. In his heart, he surmised Rose had something to do with Maren's disappearance, although he never spoke the thought out loud. But now, hearing this, witnessing the shimmering light, he let himself savor the possibility his instinct was correct.

He laid the pipe on a small table by the chair and tiptoed down the steps. No moon shone to illuminate the night as he made his way carefully toward the rock. The noisy humming and the bright light continued, as he moved closer and closer, stealthy as a cat.

The back was dark, rough, and looked like any other giant boulder. Drake crouched there straining to hear the words. He couldn't make them out, so he moved to one side, but the illumination bled around to the side, and he jumped back. *Can't get caught before I find out what this is.*

The chant continued although muffled. Once again, he peeked around the side and decided he couldn't be seen, so inched closer.

The voice was clearer and had a familiar ring.

A little bolder now, he crawled low toward the front and stretched to catch a glimpse.

Rose!

That, in itself, was a revelation, but when he shifted his gaze to the ocean he was shocked to see the object of her chant.

Bathed in the opalescent light was the most beautiful creature he'd ever laid eyes on. Half woman, half fish. A glorious mermaid. Her long, purple, silver-streaked hair floated around her like a halo, she was upright, the scales on her tail sparkling with every color of the rainbow. A crystal crown sat upon her head. Bright beams shot from her eyes, piercing the night. She was naked above the tail, her breasts full, and a necklace encircled her white neck. A majestic, midnight blue stone glowed in the center of a gorgeous amulet-like setting. Her hands were outstretched as Rose continued the chant.

My God!

Rose was still out of his sight, but her voice was clear. "Your Highest Queen, thank you for responding to my summons. I need your help."

He listened as a high-pitched chirping sound emanated from the Queen's mouth, but miraculously translated into words he could understand.

"Daughter of the sea, a summons is a last effort and only executed in the direst circumstances. I trust you have exhausted every other measure to resolve your dilemma."

Rose's voice went from strong and clear to fearful. "My Queen, as you know I've tried for many years to find a permanent vessel in which to store my soul, so I may live on land, to no avail. Betrayal is always the outcome, and I am relegated back to the sea each year, only to start anew in my quest. I've found such a vessel and have her sequestered on *The Lost Opal*. I have also found the man to which I will give my love to secure my future. But he resists. I tried a love potion, but made a mistake, and it only incited a sexual response. I am at a loss as to how to entice this man. Can you give me counsel?"

Electricity filled the air and a turbulent wind swirled around the mermaid, her eyes shooting fire.

The night turned black and ominous and left Drake afraid for his life.

The queen shouted with the ferocity of a tornado. "You dare summon me for such a frivolous and selfish request? The code of an Oceana mermaiden is to comfort the seafarers and shelter them during a storm. But you…you think only of yourself and put in peril innocent souls. I shall not help you but ban you from our midst. You may never return to the peacefulness of The Oceana Pod. You are an evil siren, not fit to call yourself a part of our community. She pointed directly at Rose.

"Your time will end on the pink moon

And return to dust at the cry of the loon."

The intensity of the 'storm' continued for a few minutes, then the Queen disappeared into the sea taking the light with her.

All was quiet, the night restored to its previous calm. Waves lapped gently onto the shore with no sign of the spectacle of a few moments ago.

He waited. Didn't flinch a muscle after the ominous edict declared by the Queen. He didn't have to wait long for Rose's response.

"No," she shouted at the empty sea. "You cannot abandon me. I need more time."

The light was gone now, so he inched forward to peek around the rock.

Rose sunk to her knees, covered her face with both hands while gut-wrenching sobs shook her body.

Again, he waited.

She finally stopped crying and struggled to stand. After a final look toward the sea, she made the journey back to her cabin, head down, wiping away tears.

He watched until she disappeared unable to process what he just witnessed. *It's one thirty in the morning. Maybe this is all a dream. But the waves are making their whooshing sound as they pound into the beach, a dog barks in the distance, and the stars dance in the sky. No, this is no dream. I did see Rose beseech a mermaid for help and I heard the Queen's edict that Rose's time is at an end at the beginning of the pink moon. If I remember right, the pink moon indicates spring. That's just two weeks from now.*

On the trek back to his cabin, he remembered Malcolm who probably was beside himself by now. He opened the door and the dog bounded out and down the steps heading straight for Passion Rock.

"There's nothing there, boy. The show is all over."

Malcolm sniffed around, yipping, obviously sensing something, but hurried back when he came up empty.

"Good boy. Now let's get some sleep. It'll take me some time to figure this out. Is Rose a mermaid? Does she have Maren stashed on something called *The Lost Opal*? Am I the guy she mentioned? Come on, Malcolm, help me out here."

The canine looked up at his master and whined.

How I wish he could talk. With his senses, he's bound to know something I don't.

The whiskey bottle stood on the end table where he left it. He noticed his shaking hands as he reached for it. *No one will believe me if I tell them what happened, but now I have a clue as to where Maren might be.*

He poured a measure of the smooth and calming alcohol

and gulped it down, emptying the glass. A shiver went through him as the whiskey found its way into his bloodstream. *Now to find out about this Lost Opal.*

His laptop sat on the counter in the kitchen. He retrieved the computer and searched for anything he could find about *The Lost Opal*. To his surprise a sailing vessel of the seventeen hundreds popped up right away. His voice was hushed as he spoke, "The seventeen hundreds? How can Maren be on that thing. It couldn't still be around."

He scrolled down to check if any more vessels carried the name. Nothing. Only the one mentioned in the seventeen hundreds. The description said a wooden vessel with voluminous masts and sails. "No way it survived this long."

One by one, he went over what he could remember of what Rose said to the so-called 'Queen of the Mermaids.' "Maren is stashed on *The Lost Opal*; she found the man she wanted to love her. A potion was involved but had no effect." He continued speaking out loud, "That had to be me. Thank God, I was immune to her trickery. What else? …The 'Queen' rejected her request and banned her from the 'pod.' Is that what they call a gathering of mermaids? Must be."

The whiskey relaxed him; his eyes closed. "I need to sleep. Maybe when I wake up I'll see all this in a different light."

Rose entered her cabin, shut the door, and leaned against it, overwhelmed with grief and loss. *She banned me. I cannot go back to the pod. What will happen at the pink moon? Will I die? Her words were: 'Your time will end on the pink moon and return to dust at the cry of the loon.'* Desperation engulfed her. She pushed away from the door and plopped into her plush chair. *I'm alone.*

She sat in the darkness for a while, sifting through the

knowledge of the centuries stored within her. As the night progressed to morning, she resolved to continue her quest with or without the help of 'The Queen.' *The Book of Spells* was in her possession. *I'll just keep trying, studying until I find the right spell. I haven't much time.*

The chapter for love potions fell open almost at will. One by one, she studied them, eliminating those not suited to her situation. The thick book contained hundreds of spells. She'd stolen the copy. For over a hundred years it remained in her possession leaving her to assume no one suspected her as the thief. But now, the angry Queen might put two and two together and come after her for the volume.

Frustrated at not finding the specific spell, she slammed the book shut. *I refuse to give up. Everything is in place. Maren is out of the picture. Drake's attraction is obvious. All I have to do is convince him to love me.*

She rose and inspected her face in the living room's gilded mirror. *I am still beautiful. My figure is perfect as attested by Drake's attention. He's halfway there. Surely, it won't take much to secure his love. Spell or no spell, he's mine.*

CHAPTER TWELVE

A DULL THUD WOKE MAREN. "WHAT WAS THAT?" SHE bolted upright, immediately blinded by the sun streaming through the bay window. She blinked a couple of times, then remembered *The Book of Spells* she'd been reading when sleep claimed her. A quick search of her lap revealed the nature of the noise. The book had fallen to the floor.

I have many questions for the captain. I must hurry. In her haste she wiggled into the slippers, but on the wrong feet, corrected the mistake, grabbed the book, and hastened to dress.

Before she jerked the door open she looked down, laughed, and said, "Whoops, I still have my slippers on. For Pete's sake, I need to slow down." She changed into a pair of sneakers the captain provided, then dashed out to find him.

The mouth-watering aroma of bacon led her to the kitchen, where he was bent over the stove flipping hotcakes.

"Good morning, Maren. Did you sleep well?" He sent one hotcake into the air with a flick of his wrist and caught the sweet-smelling cake deftly on the spatula. At the same time, he turned the sizzling bacon with a fork and didn't miss a beat.

"Do you have eyes in the back of your head? I didn't make a sound."

He turned. "Caught a whiff of the cologne I left for you. I'm glad you felt comfortable enough to use it. Hungry?"

"Famished," she replied. "It was thoughtful of you to leave the cologne for me. It's a lovely fragrance. I've never heard of it before. Listen, I want to talk to you about this…"

"No talk before we eat, my dear. They say breakfast is the most important meal of the day. We have plenty of time to discuss whatever you want." He dished up a hotcake, put a couple of pieces of bacon on the plate and slid the meal across the table. "Eat up while I pour some coffee. The syrup is warm, so help yourself. Orange juice?"

"Why yes, thank you." The chair scraped against the wooden floor as she sat down. "This smells amazing. I didn't realize how hungry I was." The book looked conspicuous on the table, but she wanted it in plain sight to watch for his reaction. Unsure he'd told her the whole truth about his exile, she wanted to see if he flinched at the sudden appearance of such an edition.

The coffee was hot and rich, the orange juice tart and cold. The hotcake slathered with butter and rich maple syrup melted in her mouth, and the bacon had just the right crunch. *Whatever he is, he sure can cook.*

Nelson sat across from her engrossed in his own meal.

She patted her mouth with a napkin and waited for him to finish.

He ate with gusto and slurped his coffee until the cup was empty. "Now what is so darn-blamed important that you wanted to skip breakfast?"

She reached over to touch the book and waited.

His gaze rested on the object. "Have you found something helpful in this book?"

"Maybe. Care to share why this is on your shelf?" She showed him the cover.

"Book of Spells," he read. "I don't recall seeing that particular publication before. Where did you find this?"

"You mean you didn't know the book was on your shelves

among your reading material? I find it hard to miss…given Rose is an evil siren. She wouldn't let something like this out of her possession. What aren't you telling me?"

He shook his head and stroked his beard. "I swear, I've told you everything about all of this. Why would I lie to you? I want out of here as much as you. Tell me where you found it."

"In your bookcase in my room. Third shelf, about eye level. I couldn't sleep, so decided to go through your books. I started at the top and worked down." She watched his face with great interest for any sign of deception. *If he is lying he certainly doesn't let his expression give him away.*

"Lass, I've read every book in that room. Multiple times over these long years. I've never come across that book."

She allowed herself a deep breath. *He's telling the truth.*

"How do you think it came to be here?" she asked.

He continued to stare at the book. A few moments passed. Finally, he reached for the volume and whispered, "She's been here recently."

"Who? Rose?"

"Had to be. She's the only one who knows where I am, she cast the spell. This was all her doing."

"So, did she leave it on purpose? Have a change of heart hoping you'd find the answer to release you from this purgatory? Maybe a taunt?" She flipped through the pages. "I went through a lot of this, but nothing makes sense to me."

"If she's been here, I sure haven't seen her. Why I'd throttle her if she appeared, you can be sure." He rose, went to the stove, and poured more coffee. "I suspect you'd have to be a sorcerer of sorts to understand how to cast a spell. But surely we can find something a lay person can do in this book. Like a beginner in the ways of deviltry. Or are they all born that way?"

"I'm sure I don't know. We need to study the whole thing.

There might be a clue inside." Her thoughts scrambled as she tried to decide how best to achieve the task.

Nelson offered a plan. "How about we take turns? I'll take a few hours, then you pick up where I left off."

Something didn't ring true about his suggestion, but she couldn't put a finger on why. "I think we need to go through the book together. Our interpretations might be different. That way we wouldn't skip over anything the other might find inconsequential."

The coffee sloshed over his cup as he sat down hard. "Maren, forgive me, but you don't seem to trust me. Your transparency is written on your face. You're suspicious. What makes you think I'd willingly exile myself to this place for all these years?"

"I…well, you see…." She stopped. "Finding the book on your shelf raised questions. Why is this particular book here? I can't believe Rose left it for you. Why did you not see the book before." Now she went to the stove and poured more coffee. "Nothing about this whole thing makes sense. So how can I believe, even in you, at this point?" She sat down lifting the cup to her lips.

His expression changed from one of defiance to sympathy. "Of course you are confused. Who wouldn't be?" He reached across the table for the book. "I don't know how this got here, but together we'll solve this."

"I'm sorry I doubted you, Captain. At this point I can't afford to ignore anything." She rose. "Let's get started then."

"Good, I'd prefer a nice sea breeze to clear our heads. Will you join me on deck?" He clutched the book and led the way.

⇒❦⇐

Henry Nelson studied The Book of Spells alongside Maren even though a bruised ego hung like a cloud over the whole operation. *Why does she mistrust me so? I've no idea how that book landed on my bookshelf. The very idea that I should impose such a fate upon myself is ludicrous.* Lost in thought he jumped at Maren's exclamation.

"Here it is!"

"What? Where?" Excitement coursed through him as he peered over her shoulder.

"This incantation deals with mermaids who want to change into a whole human and leave the sea life behind." She pointed to the text.

He scanned the verse. "Yes, this must be the one. But we'll have to study more. We don't want to repeat the spell only to find ourselves cast into a different parallel world. In my estimation, these things can be tricky if not done carefully. Do you agree?"

"Yes, we must make sure we understand what will happen. There must be more in this chapter. Maybe on how to undo a spell. That will be more to our liking. Remember, we don't want to cast a spell, we want to undo it. But what will be the ramifications?"

He slid the book in front of him and read the page. "In the spell she issued all those years ago, she mentioned a key. Have you seen anything about that in here?"

"No. I was thinking the same thing. There's more to this than just a spell. We still need to find the key. Remember the verse?

'Beware the siren's song of the sea,
Lest you're drawn like moth to flame.
For one mistake will require the key
To retrieve your soul from whence it came'"

As Maren spoke the words, black clouds gathered to block the sun and a high wind threatened to blow them both over. Lightening pierced the darkened sky in an angry cacophony.

"We struck a nerve," she shouted over the turbulent squall.

"What?" The captain cupped his ear.

She shouted louder, "I said, we've struck a nerve. We must be on the right track."

The pages fluttered violently until the book closed with a thud and the tempest ceased.

CHAPTER THIRTEEN

THE WIND STOPPED, AND THE SUDDEN STILLNESS UNNERVED Maren as a tremble rippled through her body. "Damn. What was that?"

The sun beamed brightly, and the now cloudless sky returned to its lively blue as if the storm never happened.

Nelson made a guttural sound as he stared at the leather-bound volume. He glanced at her. "Could the book do that, or did you conjure something up yourself?"

"I didn't do anything." She pointed upward. "See the sky? Not a sign of a cloud, no wind, complete calm, and did you notice the book remained steadfastly on the railing during the squall?"

"The book seems to have a life of its own, for sure. Here's a thought. We spoke the verse. Was the spell triggered because we said the passage aloud?" He reached toward the volume in question but drew back his hand.

"We can't be afraid," she encouraged. "The ticket to our freedom has to be written in here." Gingerly, she retrieved the spell book from the railing and found the chapter they'd quoted from. "As long as we don't say the words out loud, I think we're fine. I'm guessing we've much to learn."

"We need a system, Maren. The task is overwhelming and could take longer than we expect."

"Agreed. But this is our jumping off point. We begin with this chapter."

The captain looked to the sky. "I think we're safer in the galley. Let's take this downstairs before another squall dusts up."

"You're right." She followed him down the stairs, the book held tightly in her hands.

Drake Morgan woke with a start, a dream at the forefront of his mind, but fading fast. A woman with auburn hair, floating above him, a seductive smile dancing on her face. In a flash of light, she disappeared, and he was left empty and alone. He sat up expecting to find the vision lurking there somehow. "What in tarnation was that? A mermaid? Maren? No, not her because the woman's hair was a soft red, and the face wasn't right." His mind cleared a bit. "Rose?"

He squeezed his eyes shut trying to will the face back, but to no avail. The event at Passion Rock flashed in front of him. "Must be what triggered the dream."

Malcolm whined at his knee.

"Hey boy, you should have pushed the bottle out of my hand. I drank too much last night and now I'm seeing things, or at least dreaming them."

The morning was pleasant, balmy, and Malcolm bounded outside with the joy of an unburdened soul. Drake was about to follow him for their morning walk when he spotted a lone figure coming toward him. "I sure don't need a visitor this morning," he grumbled.

The dog planted all fours in a menacing way and growled in the direction of the intruder.

"Malcom, heel!"

Immediately, he returned to his master. Drake pulled him inside and shut the door.

"Damn, it's Rose. I hope she didn't see me." He peeked through the curtains as she came closer, a determined march to her step.

Malcolm woofed.

The knock was sharp and rattled the window.

He put a hand on Malcom's muzzle and remained silent hoping she'd give up and go away.

Luck would fail him.

She persisted and knocked louder. "I know you're in there, Drake. I saw you and your dog. No use avoiding me, I'm going to knock until you answer." She pounded the door again. "I mean what I say. I'll not budge from here until you open the door. We need to talk. I brought tea and pastries."

His worst nightmare unfolded in front of him. The dream lingered, confusing him as memories of the night before rushed back. He wasn't prepared to deal with her yet. *How can I make her leave? What if she has Maren? I can't let her know my suspicions though. Damn, I need a clear head.*

"Look, Rose," he shouted through the door. "I've got a hangover. Please go and come back later when I can have a civil conversation."

Rose pounded once more. "Then you're in luck. I brought an herbal tea. As it turns out, this stuff cures hangovers. Let me in and I'll brew some. You don't have to talk, just try the tea."

The pounding made him wince. Buzzing like angry bees filled his ears. But even though the noise distracted his common sense, alarms went off in his head and his patience wore thin. *I need coffee, not some dadgum tea. If that's the only way to make her leave, so be it.*

Against his better judgement, he pushed Malcolm behind him, told him to stay, and opened the door.

She shoved her way through and headed for the kitchen. "You look pitiful. This will perk you right up."

He stumbled aside. His answer was curt and nasty. "Okay, fine. While I make some strong, black coffee you can brew the tea. But I hardly think that stuff will clear my head."

Malcolm growled.

She glanced up as she filled the pot with water. "What about him?" She nodded toward the dog.

"You understand, he doesn't like you, right? Some kind of dog sense I guess. Can't do anything about that."

A smile crossed her lips. "I'm determined to make him my friend, eventually. You'll see. I have a way with animals."

I bet you do. He summoned Malcolm and ordered him to his bed.

He wasn't about to leave her alone in his kitchen, but damn, he needed a shower. He couldn't stand the smell of stale alcohol and cigarettes swirling around him. *She must leave before she conjures a spell on me. How can I get out of drinking her infernal tea?*

He turned to find her sitting on the stool, steam rising from two teacups on the bar.

She smiled kindly at him. "Come, have a taste. A surefire way to cure a hangover, guaranteed."

Afraid suspicion showed on his face and would somehow affect her leaving, he forced a smile and sat across from her. "Where did these come from? I don't have teacups, only coffee mugs."

"I figured as much, so I brought mine. Tea drinking is for an acquired palette and should be done with the proper implements. Sugar or cream?" she asked indicating the bowl of sugar cubes and a tiny pot full of cream.

"Is it called black if you don't use either?"

Her laugh put him temporarily at ease.

"No, just *plaine* as the French say." The word rolled off her tongue.

She doesn't seem so evil this morning. "French, huh. Okay, *plaine*." His tongue didn't want to cooperate. "You speak the language?"

After a tiny sip from her cup, she replied, "I speak many languages. And may I say, there is a lot you don't know about me."

He avoided looking into her eyes. Aware of what she is, he proceeded with an abundance of caution. "True. Nor do you have a clue about me." *I don't think she saw me last night. I'm hoping this really is about Maren and not a feeble attempt to put me under her spell.*

"Oh, I know more than you think. Now drink your tea. It's quite tasty."

The cup felt fragile in his calloused hand, but he managed to pick it up. He sniffed the liquid, decided it was okay, and took a sip. "Not bad. There's a kind of chicory flavor to it."

"Yes, among other things. Drink it down, then you can have your coffee." She studied him closely.

"You mean, in one gulp?" *God, I hope I don't regret this.*

"Yes, the cup is small, should be a one swallow event for a big man like you."

He nodded and put the cup to his lips. *Here goes! At least the flavor isn't bad and if it will get rid of her, fine. I survived her last attempt to drug me. Maybe I'll get lucky again.*

In one gulp he polished it off. Before he put the cup down, writing appeared at the bottom. "What's this? A prophecy in a teacup, like a fortune cookie? This word looks French. What does it mean? *Empoisonné*."

"You need to brush up on your French, my dear captain." She rose, placed her teacup and accruements in her bag, leaving his cup on the counter, and went to the door. "I'll leave you to your coffee, Drake. Dinner at my house tonight. At seven. And don't be late."

He watched her leave, relieved she went so quickly. "What

the hell. Why would she think I would have dinner with her? What a laugh. Not a chance, Malcolm. We're bachelors and we're going to stay that way." He reached for the teacup and started after her but changed his mind. After turning it around and around in his hand, he fastened his interest on the French word. *Empoisonné. Now what the hell does that mean?*

Bleary-eyed, he went to his computer instead of his cell phone, typed in the word, and clicked translate. A jolt ran through his body as he stared at the word emblazoned across the screen.

Poisoned!

As he stared at the teacup, the shocking word faded slowly from the bottom of the cup, leaving him to wonder if he'd actually seen it at all.

He patted himself up and down. *I don't feel weird, nothing is happening. Am I paranoid or will there be a delayed reaction of some kind?*

Malcolm left his bed and whimpered at his knee.

"Catch me if I fall, old boy."

CHAPTER FOURTEEN

Maren poured over *The Book of Spells* while Captain Nelson paced the galley floor.

Every once in a while he stopped and asked, "Find anything?"

She'd shake her head and keep reading, mouthing the words silently, careful not to verbalize anything.

He poured another cup of coffee, slamming the pot on the stove. "I'll be hornswoggled, Maren. We've been at this for hours. If there was something in this book to free us we'd have found it by now."

A deep sigh released the tension in her body. She sat back; shoulders slumped. "I'm afraid you might be right. I simply can't make heads or tails of this gibberish. We're definitely missing something." She stood and stretched with a yawn. "Do you think that whole weather event was only a coincidence?"

He stroked his beard. "I've been wondering that myself. We got so caught up in that infernal book we automatically assumed the connection. What shall we do now?"

"Take a break, I say. My eyes are bleary. I must go topside for some air. You coming?" she asked.

"Aye, plenty of time before we need to fix lunch. I think a nice stroll around the deck will help clear the fog from my brain."

Maren led the way up the wooden stairway.

A few white wind-driven clouds drifted to the west, adorning the baby blue sky.

Under her breath, she said, "What I'd give to be one of those clouds, drifting my way home."

"Did you say something?" the captain asked.

"Just mumbling to myself. Wishing I was a cloud floating away from here."

"How are you holding up, Maren? You've been here a week now. You're not giving up are you?"

"Of course not. Not in my nature." She pointed down the galley stairs. "The stupid book got me off track. I'm thinking it was a diversion tactic put here by Rose to keep us off balance and headed in the wrong direction. Think about it. She wouldn't leave her book here for us to find the answer."

Nelson clasped his hands behind his back and paced. "You're probably right. She's a down-right devious one." He stopped and faced her. "So, what's the next step?"

"We keep looking, keep thinking. Try to figure out how Rose's mind works." The light breeze made her sleepy. She rubbed her eyes. "Think I'll close my eyes for a bit. What's for lunch?"

"Biscuits and eggs, I think. Any objections?"

"Perfect. I love your biscuits. Wake me in an hour." She headed toward her room and closed the door behind her.

Once inside, she plopped on the bed and covered her face with both hands. *Something's not right. What am I missing? The chant played like a broken record in her mind.*

'Beware the siren's song of the sea,
Lest you're drawn like moth to flame.
For one mistake will require the key
To retrieve your soul from whence it came'.

She lay down and whispered, hands still over her face. "A key? What can it be, an actual key or a clue of some sort?"

As she relaxed, her body went limp, and she drifted into a light slumber.

You'll never find it, Maren dear. I've hidden it well. Drake will soon be mine and you will live out your days on this miserable ship. You might as well make the best of it. I certainly will.

She woke with a start as a demonic laugh filled the room.

A mist floated above her but dissolved instantly.

"Rose!"

She scrambled upright and hurried out on deck to find the captain. Her foot caught on a coil of rope, and she fell flat. A groan escaped as she assessed her injuries. A bump on the head, scraped knees and elbows, but otherwise, not much damage. "Serves me right for trying to hurry," she moaned.

Once on her feet, she made her way to the galley stairway. *I must tell Captain Nelson about my dream.* She called his name as she took the steps one at a time. Normally she'd smell the aroma of the biscuits, but nothing tickled her nose this time. She shouted again, "Captain. I have something to tell you. Rose…"

He wasn't there.

Nothing was cooking. The counters were clean. There wasn't even coffee brewing.

He got distracted. Must be topside. She headed toward the stairs but stopped to glance at the table. "The book is gone," she shouted then hurried up to the deck and called once more, "Captain. Where are you?"

Only silence. Her chest clenched as fear gripped her. *I don't sense him anywhere. Has Rose taken him, leaving me here alone? Oh God, please not that!*

After a frantic search above deck, she scrambled below, looking in every hold, every nook and cranny. As she turned away from the last room, she heard a muffled sound and followed it to a closet, barricaded by crates.

In a frenzy, she tossed the wooden boxes aside and rattled the door.

Probably locked from the inside. She called his name while looking for something to jimmy the door. A beat-up bucket full of various tools sat in a corner. She went through them in desperation until she came upon a crowbar. *Perfect.* It took a while, but eventually, the lock broke, and the door opened.

"Captain," she cried.

He was gagged, hands tied behind his back, feet bound with heavy ropes. His eyes bulged and he mumbled behind the gag.

"Hold on." She tore the cloth from his mouth. "Who did this?"

He sputtered and choked, but finally said, "Rose. She was here. I went downstairs to start lunch when she appeared. She didn't say a word, just smiled. And poof, I was down here bound and gagged."

Her fingers picked at the rope binding his hands. "I'm sure I saw her, too. It was like a mist or something, but she didn't tie me up. Just laughed at me and quoted the chant, then disappeared."

He nodded as he peered over his shoulder at her attempt to untie him.

Eventually, the thick cordage loosened enough for her to tackle the knot and it fell away.

He groaned as he moved his arms forward.

"You're gonna have to help me with your feet. My fingers are darn near bloody," she said.

He rubbed both arms vigorously, then deftly untied his feet. "She's playing with us. She must be confident her plan is working. I've not known her to do anything like this before."

She helped him stand. "The book. Do you have it?"

"No, it was still on the table when she appeared."

"I hate to say this, but it's gone. She took the blame thing, I guess."

The captain had trouble walking as they stumbled up the stairs. He'd been down there for over an hour while she napped.

"Once the blood starts flowing again, I'll be right as rain. Just give me a few minutes."

Back in the galley Maren sat him down. "I'll make lunch. She didn't harm me, and you need to rest."

He nodded back to her with a slight grin. "This time, I'll let you."

While she started the coffee, she asked him some questions about his recipe for the biscuits. She followed it to the letter, slid them into the oven, and poured them each a cup of brew. After the caffeine fortified her soul, she broke several eggs in a pan. "Do you think she'll try something else, or will she leave us to rot?"

He sipped Maren's version of coffee and shook his head. "She's not done with us yet, Maren. She has a vengeful nature. I wouldn't be surprised to find some other nasty 'lesson' for us to learn." He stared into his cup.

She watched him study the mug then turned to pull the biscuits out of the oven. "What are you thinking?"

"I'm a bit worried about your Captain. Drake isn't it?"

"Yes, Drake Morgan. I've thought about him, too. What if he doesn't play by her rules, so to speak. What can she do to him?"

"She can do what she's done to us. Or worse. From your description of him and the events you've told me about, he sounds like a likeable chap. I'd hate to see harm come to him if he jilts her in any way." He sliced a biscuit and slathered butter over it.

"She'd ban him here?" she asked.

"Oh no, I doubt that. She'd find another vessel where he'd be alone. That's what has me worried."

She cut her eyes toward him. "Another vessel? Can she do that…I mean summon a ship at will? I ask because he doesn't have one of his own right now, not like you. *The Lost Opal* is yours, so it stands to reason why she'd strand you here. But Drake—? How does that work?"

He settled his kindly gaze on her and spoke with a gentle tone, "She can do whatever the bloody hell she wants to, Maren. She's wicked and has the power. If I were to guess, I'd say she'd choose a derelict craft though. His punishment if he doesn't bend to her will is likely to be severe."

She held his gaze and declared, "That's it, then. We've got to locate that ship before she sends him there. If I know Drake, he won't go along with any of this. He'll buck her at the first opportunity."

A grimace settled on his face. "May I remind you, dearie. We're stuck here. We don't have the ability to find anything, much less a ship hundreds of years old."

"Sure, but what I mean is finding something in your logbooks or other books in your library. Maybe we can pinpoint where she might send him, find a way to save him."

The frown deepened accenting the wrinkles etched on his sailor's face. "Even if we did find such a boat, what could we do?"

"I don't know, but in the course of our search maybe we'd come across something to help us figure out this mess." She looked imploringly at him. "We have to try, Captain Nelson, we have to try."

CHAPTER FIFTEEN

"**W**HAT ARE MY OPTIONS?" DRAKE WHISPERED TO THE empty room. As a Navy man he was used to regulation, although he no longer held a position in the esteemed profession. "Calm objectivity needs to prevail. Maren's been missing for a week. The police haven't found any clues. Will they simply sweep her disappearance under the rug?"

He grabbed his coffee mug, went outside, leaned against the porch post, and studied the rhythm of the sea. *Option one: I can do nothing. Option two: I can go back and bug the cops. Option three: I can put a chokehold on Rose until she tells me what she did with Maren.*

The waves crashed on the shore, soothing, but at the same time leaving an uncomfortable hollow in his belly. *She's out there somewhere, I feel it.*

After a while, he settled in the porch chair with Malcolm at his feet. He pondered the tea incident and Rose's confidence he would appear for dinner this evening. *Of course, I'm not going. Or should I? She tried to use the power of persuasion with the tea-cup. I'm not poisoned, or I'd have some sort of reaction. Mind games. She's playing me. So, I…*

Malcolm stood and growled at almost the same time movement caught the peripheral of his vision.

Drake rose and stared at Maren's cabin. "Whoa boy, something's going on over there. Let's go check it out."

He set his mug on the side table, grabbed the leash, secured Malcolm, and together they crossed the damp sand to find out who lurked about the empty bungalow. As they approached, he recognized Telsa Stewart, Maren's editor. She lugged a suitcase from the back of what appeared to be a dark gray Acura SUV.

"Can I help you, Ms. Stewart?" he called out. "I saw something moving over here and hoped it was Maren."

Telsa jumped and dropped the luggage. "Oh, you startled me. Drake, isn't it? I'm sorry, but I can't remember your last name."

He hurried over to retrieve the bag and followed her to the porch. "Morgan, ma'am. Drake Morgan. I hate to rush you, but have you heard anything from Maren?"

The surprised expression disappeared from her face instantly, replaced with a furrow between her brows and a frown. "Why no. That's why I came. The police tell me they haven't any leads. I'm beyond frustrated." She pushed her black curls to one side and pointed to the rest of her luggage piled on the deck."

He placed the suitcase on top of the others. "You plan to stay awhile?"

She crossed her arms and looked him directly in the eye. "Do you have a problem with that?"

He raised his hands in defense. "Oh no, ma'am, not at all. In fact, I'm glad you're here. If we can, I'd like to work together to find her. Mind you, she and I barely know one another, but I developed a bit of a connection with her. I'm worried she's not okay. When you have time, I'd like to compare information."

Her body relaxed as she sunk into a chair. "I'm sorry. Wasn't trying to be difficult. It's…well, no one's concerned! I understand she was only a visitor here, not a native to the area, but she's a human, and she disappeared on this beach. Shouldn't somebody care?"

He reached for her hand and dropped to one knee beside her. "I care." In a swift motion, he stood and pulled her to her feet. "You look as though you need a jolt of caffeine. You know your way around a coffee pot, right? My first cup of morning coffee is over there." He gestured toward his cabin. "Didn't finish it. Heaven knows, I need more than one cup. Could you make us some while I take these bags inside?"

A smile brightened her face. "Oh, that's a wonderful idea. Yes, I'll make coffee. Are you sure you want to wrestle those? I packed for a month."

"Piece of cake." He lifted the top one, opened the screen, and stepped aside while she went in first.

One by one, he retrieved the luggage and deposited them neatly in the bedroom. By the time he finished, the ambrosial aroma of roasted beans drifted through the cabin.

"All bags present and accounted for, ma'am. Coffee smells great," Drake kept his voice light and cheerful. *Plenty of time to get to the serious discussion after she gathers her thoughts and isn't so frazzled.*

Telsa placed two mugs on the bar and smiled. "You showed up at just the right time. I can't thank you enough. Now, I can unpack at leisure and think about what my next step will be. Maren's target date has passed, so I know something bad has happened to her. She never misses a deadline. I need an ally and you fit the bill." She sat on the bar stool and sipped cautiously from the steaming cup.

He removed his cap, placed it on the bar, and studied her face. She was more relaxed now; a calm aster blue replaced the fear that lurked in her eyes a few moments ago.

"I have much to tell you, Ms. Stewart. Some of it you might find a bit hard to swallow."

"Please, call me Telsa. And may I call you Drake?" she asked.

"Yes, of course. Telsa then. To begin with, I guess, I should ask if you believe in paranormal events. There's no point in going on unless you have an open mind about such things." He watched her carefully for any shock about the subject he was about to embark on.

She didn't flinch.

"Paranormal events. You mean she's a victim of a metaphysical encounter? I'm as open-minded as the next person, so I'll give your explanation my full attention. Is that why the police have no leads, nor any desire to pursue this?"

After a strong gulp of hot coffee, he shook his head. "Not exactly. I should begin at the beginning for you to understand completely. Have you heard much about Passion Rock? The rock Maren's footprints led to."

She shrugged. "Not much. It's big, it's by the water, and that's where they think she disappeared."

"You met Rose, right?"

She squinted. "Uh, yes, why?" The caution in her voice was unmistakable.

A soft laugh preceded his answer. "I see you are skeptical of our friend, Rose. As am I."

Her gaze relaxed. "Good to know. There's something about the woman that doesn't ring true. Does she have something to do with Maren's disappearance?"

"Do you want to hear the whole story?"

She nodded. "Yes, all of it."

Drake took his time sharing his experiences with Rose. He began from the time she barged into his cabin when Maren was there, how Malcolm always growled when she was around, her attempt to get him drunk, and the scene at Passion Rock and the Queen Mermaid. He ended with the teacup and *Empoisonné* emblazoned across the bottom.

"She's ordered me to dinner tonight. Not sure what I'll do."

She listened until he finished with no visible expression on her face.

He picked up his mug and peered at her before he took a sip. "Do you think I'm crazy?"

Like a deflated balloon, she sighed and leaned back. "No, I don't think that. It is a little far-fetched but in a strange way makes sense. It doesn't appear you had any adverse effects from the tea. None that shows, anyway. So, what is your next move? Are you going to dinner tonight?"

He shrugged. "Haven't a clue."

Hesitation preempted her reply.

When she didn't say anything, he set his mug down. "What do you think I should do?"

She leaned forward again, but responded with continued reticence, "All this hocus-pocus brings a bit of validation to what I felt when I left here last week." She flushed a bit as if embarrassed. "I was overcome by an urge to leave. My mind told me to stay and search for Maren, but the compulsion to go home won out." She dropped a sugar cube into her coffee. "When I arrived home, the impulse wore off. That's why I'm back. I've only been here an hour or so and I don't have that inclination to take off like before. Yet."

"You think Rose put some sort of spell on you?" Drake offered.

"I'm not saying that for sure. I'm an open-minded individual. I have to be to survive in the publishing business. But mermaids and spells, well, that's not exactly where my brain lives. You're a down to earth guy, probably not prone to vivid imagination, but you are a sailor. You've seen things the rest of us will never witness. I've got to see it for myself, I guess."

"I have an idea. Come with me tonight. Let's surprise Rose. She might have something up her sleeve for me, but she won't be expecting you. She won't have time to concoct something to put you out of commission. What do you say?"

"Show up uninvited?" She shook her head. "I'm not sure…."

"We want to find Maren, don't we? I've resisted her attempts before. I'll protect you," he insisted.

She studied his face.

He could envision the wheels turning in her mind.

Finally, she said, "Okay. I'll go. What time tonight?"

"Seven."

"Perfect, I can unpack and rest some."

"I'll pick you up at six. We can walk to her house, line up a strategy of some sort." He stood, rinsed his cup in the sink, and moved to the door. "See you later. And thanks. I feel good about us teaming up."

Rose looked at the clock on her mantle. "Seven hours before Drake arrives. He doesn't realize it yet, but he'll be in my power before midnight. I have much planned for him and our future together."

After a quick check in the mirror to admire her smooth complexion and ample bosom, she went to assess her dinner preparations. This time, she wasn't taking any chances. The small cauldron bubbled on the stovetop. The spices for the spell will permeate throughout everything on the menu. From the prime rib to the potatoes, to the drinks. *All of it. Every morsel he consumes will have the ingredients needed to compel him to fall in love with me.*

"You are mine this time, Drake Morgan."

CHAPTER SIXTEEN

MAREN STOOD AT THE RAILING OF THE OLD SHIP AND watched the waves roll in, then subside. The day was warm and sunny, not a cloud in the sky. The calm rhythm of the sea belied the turmoil churning in her soul. The thought of Captain Morgan lost to Rose's vengeful heart disturbed her. *I'm so helpless. If I can't find a way off this ship, Drake is doomed. We all are.*

Henry Nelson retired to his quarters after lunch, succumbing to the after-effects of the encounter with Rose.

Maren didn't like being the solitary figure on the deck. It made her uneasy, but she recognized his need for rest. She turned toward the sun to soak in its warmth as she pondered how to free them from this purgatory. The word 'key' resurfaced in her mind. *I remember it was mentioned in the chant, but I can't help thinking it's a physical object, a sort of clue. Where can it be hidden? I've missed something.*

The library beckoned her, and she decided to take advantage of the captain's absence to search the books once more. She started at the top and methodically went over each one, hoping to find *The Book of Spells* or some other reference to help them. She came up empty and returned to the deck.

The water lapped against the side of the ship, rhythmic, hypnotic, restoring a calm in her soul so lacking these days. Her eyelids drooped as she listened to the restorative tempo of the sea until a flash of light revived her attention.

Something in the distance shimmered on the water. She squinted into the sun, shaded her eyes with one hand, and tried to identify the object. It was too far away, but it stayed there, sort of dancing on the surface, its mass glimmering in the light. *Reminds me of Passion Rock, except there was a high-pitched sound, too.*

Just as the thought passed through her consciousness, an eerie wail sounded faintly from the direction of what could only be described as a mirage. There was no other explanation since they were in limbo here with no contact from the outside world.

The hair on her arms stood up at the sound, and chills rippled her skin. *It sounds as if it's calling out. A name perhaps?*

It came in waves. Two syllables. Aaaa…nnnn. Over and over. Aaaa…nnnn. She cupped one ear hoping to enhance the sound. She stood quite still fearing any movement might make this apparition disappear as it had at Passion Rock.

To her surprise the phantasm moved closer, and the sound increased.

That's when she heard it plainly.

"Ma-ren. Ma-ren."

She stiffened. "What? Surely I didn't hear that right." Her words drifted over the water like a scarf loose in the wind.

The captain's voice made her turn around.

"You heard it right, Maren." He touched her shoulder like a father soothes a child. "They are calling for you."

She turned again to face the sea. "Who is calling me? Why?"

Captain Nelson joined her at the railing. "The mermaids. I've never seen this phenomenon before, but I remember my father talking about it. Of all the women who Rose banished to the ship, this is the first time they've called for anyone."

"I've heard the stories of mermaid's saving ships, how for the most part, they are good, not evil." She shook her head. "I didn't believe them really, until Rose. So, why are they calling me?"

He stroked his beard, continuing to stare at the mirage-like phenomenon. "I don't rightly know, lass. This catches me by surprise, too. Let's see what happens."

They stood shoulder to shoulder watching, listening.

The apparition drifted closer. The sing-song melody sweet on her ear; the sound of her name now clear and welcoming.

"What should I do?" she whispered.

"Just wait," he said, his voice low and reverential. "They'll tell you."

As they moved closer, their appearance became more defined until she could make out their long, almost turquoise hair floating around bewitching facial features. Three of them. Indescribable beauty, ethereal, arms outstretched, and singing in perfect harmony while calling her name.

She stood transfixed until they stopped about a half a mile from the ship.

"They're beautiful," she said.

As they waited, the water parted, and another ascended in front of the others.

She gasped at the exceptional beauty of this one. Same long hair, but the color was something she'd never seen before. A deep purple with streaks of silver throughout. A crystal crown rested on top of her head and an amulet of deep blue graced her naked breasts. "I greet you in friendship, Maren Raybourn."

Thunderstruck, she stared at the beautiful creature before her.

Captain Nelson nudged her with his elbow.

She whispered, "How do you know my name?"

The mermaid ignored the question. "May I come aboard?"

The captain answered this time. "You are more than welcome to board this ship."

Before she could imagine how in the world the half woman, half fish would accomplish this task, the mermaid disappeared in a whirling mist. She shed her watery persona and reappeared on the deck fully draped in a white gossamer dress which clung to her like a second skin and revealed the outline of her very womanly legs.

"Oh, my goodness," Maren murmured and could only stare in disbelief.

Nelson reached out to take the mermaid's hand and welcome her to the ship.

She ignored the captain's gesture. When she spoke, the sound was like a dolphin's chirp or whale sounds, yet they understood every word.

"My name is Cecella, Queen of the Mermaids. I have come to warn you."

The captain chuckled, "I'm afraid you are about over two hundred years late. That's how long I've been held on this ship moored in the middle of nowhere." He pointed to Maren. "As for this little lass, she's had about a week to get used to her new surroundings. Can it be you have come to warn her?"

Again, the Queen did not answer the question, but instead issued a chant:

'If from this curse you will be free
A moonbeam will reveal the key.
Your hands on the portal must be
To repeat this mantra times three'.
Oslobodi me, naredujem ti
(Release me I command you)
Cecella repeated the chant.

Maren gasped at the prospect of finding the key. "But what is the key?" she cried.

Cecella smiled while the chirping noise filled their ears and a clear message transpired.

"In plain sight the key resides.
A precious tear from Zeus's eye."

The mist swirled around her once more and in the blink of an eye the Queen was gone.

As the sea parted to engulf Cecella, the other three mermaids drifted away and disappeared.

"Did that just happen?" Maren muttered.

The captain's voice was hushed and reverent. "I believe it did, my child."

"Can you remember the chant? We need to write it down, so we won't forget it. And the last thing she said, something about a tear from Zeus's eye." Maren's excitement shook her whole body. "I think she just gave us the way out of here."

CHAPTER SEVENTEEN

DRAKE FASTENED THE LAST BUTTON ON HIS ONLY CLEAN dress shirt as a knock sounded lightly on the door. He slicked back his wet hair and grabbed a growling Malcolm. *Dagnabit. Who can that be? I need to pick up Telsa and I'm late.*

He clipped the leash onto Malcolm's collar as a grumble continued to vibrate through the dog's chest. "Whoa, Malcolm. Let's find out who this is before you decide to take a chunk out of someone's leg."

As he pushed the dog behind him, he opened the door. "I'm busy right now…Telsa!"

"Hello, Drake. Thought I'd save you a hike in the wet sand. There's a bit of a drizzle coming down."

He blinked a couple of times and looked beyond her. "Oh, how thoughtful. You're right, and it's more than a drizzle. We should take my Jeep. Come and dry off. Malcolm won't bite—unless I tell him." He chuckled.

A frown and raised eyebrows expressed a dubious look as she peered around Drake at the dog. "Funny."

He felt the whip-like slash of Malcom's tail wagging against his leg. "Hey, he stopped growling, and his tail is going ninety to nothing. He likes you."

Telsa stepped inside and offered a hand for Malcolm to sniff. "He's beautiful. I think he remembers me from this morning."

Drake took her raincoat and indicated the kitchen. "Malcolm is a good judge of character. We've time to talk and enjoy a hot cup of coffee before we go."

"Sounds good. I'm a bit chilly," she said.

They sat at the island, the steaming mugs warming their hands.

He pushed the sugar and cream closer to her. "I'm really glad you're going with me. Rose can be a handful and I want a witness in case she tries something."

She shook her head at the offer. "I need it black tonight. Tell me more about this dinner. What can I expect?"

He set his cup down and gazed out the window. "She'll try something, but I really have no clue. What I do know is the Queen of the Mermaids said her time is almost up and mentioned the Pink Moon. That's about two weeks away. If she can't find a man to fall for her, it sounded as if she would simply disappear. That's why I'm concerned." *Am I her target?* He pulled his attention back to Telsa. "She put the spell on Maren. So—does that mean she is lost if Rose disappears? That's one reason I decided to go."

"And you think she's just going to come right out and tell you?" Telsa folded her arms and gave a lop-sided grin.

"I'm not kidding myself about that, but maybe with you along she'll slip up. I may tell her how much I've seen. That the jig is up."

They sat for a few more minutes and discussed their game plan. He wouldn't back down if she was unhappy with Telsa being there. He'd press for answers about Maren. She'd try to pick up on anything out of the ordinary in his behavior. They agreed the car keys would be safer in Telsa's bag in case he was rendered immobile.

"I never in a million years thought I'd be talking about how to subdue a mermaid or dodge a spell. This is so bizarre," she said.

He pulled on his jacket, grabbed his keys, and handed Telsa her raincoat. "I understand. Sometimes I think this is all a dream and I'll wake up to find Maren back in her cabin. But until I do, we'll proceed with this plan."

They remained quiet on the short jaunt to Rose's cabin, the only sound the swish of the wipers.

Drake pulled into the drive, turned off the motor, undid the seatbelt, and took a deep breath. "Ready?"

"As I'll ever be," she said.

He came around to assist her, but before he could shut the door, Rose shouted from the porch.

"What is this, Drake? Why is she here?"

Drake handed her his car keys, took Telsa's arm, and guided her toward the cabin, the rain making a rhythmic patter on the plastic coat. "You remember Telsa, don't you? Maren's editor. She came in today to talk to the police and ask their progress in the case. Hope you don't mind, but I thought three heads were better than two."

Rose glared at the interloper. "I suppose."

When the two arrived on the porch deck, Rose did nothing to welcome Telsa.

"Have you changed your mind about dinner?" Drake asked. "We can go into town if you like. I'll pay."

"No, I've made plenty. Come in." Rose stomped through the front door, her back an unmistakable rebuff.

He whispered to Telsa, "Here we go."

Inside, Rose continued her annoyed performance. "You're dripping all over my floor. Can't you see the coatrack in the corner?"

Telsa apologized and offered, "If you'll bring me a mop, I'll clean it up." She wriggled out of her coat and hung it on the aforementioned rack.

Rose whirled away to the kitchen but muttered, "No need. Sit down where you can find a place. I'll be right back."

Telsa asked Drake, "Should I go offer to help in the kitchen? Make sure she doesn't poison us."

He shook his head. "I think that will annoy her even more. Just eat and drink the minimum in case she's added something."

Telsa nodded.

Rose emerged from the kitchen with a tray of steaming mugs. A smile graced her lips this time. "I thought we could all use a nice warm drink. It's tea. Remember Drake?" She shifted her attention to Telsa. "I introduced him to the pleasure of a warm cup of tea this morning."

A blustery snort came from his lips, "How could I forget, Rose. Disappearing poison threat. Very funny."

She set the tea on the coffee table and smiled. "No harm, no foul, I say. Don't be mad. It was a little joke to show you another side of my personality." She focused on Telsa. "I'll be blunt. I have my cap set for Drake." A flirty laugh added to the sparkle in her eyes. "Just fair warning, Ms. Stewart. You understand, I'm sure."

Telsa's stoic face formed a disapproving frown. "I care nothing about your pursuit of Captain Morgan. I'm simply here to find out what I can about Maren's disappearance."

Rose sputtered at the rebuff, "You both are so serious. I was only trying to lighten the mood. Maren is of the utmost importance to me, I…"

Morgan interrupted, "Cut it out, Rose. We're here about Maren, so I'll come right to the point. You know exactly what happened to her, I'm sure of it."

The glare in Rose's eyes took Drake back a step. For the first time, he actually saw the evil in her gaze.

"You're treading on dangerous ground. If you pursue this line of thought, you'll be sorry," she said, her voice low and vicious.

"I was there that night—when the Queen of the Mermaids made her appearance, and you pitched your sad plea for her to help you snare me."

Rose stood; shock replaced the evil persona. Her nostrils flared, a red flush spread from her neck to both cheeks, and eyes as wild as a cornered buck stared down at him. "You…you were there? How dare you eavesdrop."

"Eavesdrop, Rose? You did little to hide the encounter. Anyone on the beach had a front row seat."

Rose's words slid from her lips like a snake's hiss. "What are you talking about?"

He rose to face her. "I was behind Passion Rock and stayed out of sight until the Queen disappeared. I know your plan and that you have less than two weeks to complete this diabolical plot. The only thing I can focus on is Maren." He took a step toward her and spat. "Where is she?"

Shock melted from her face and her eyes turned to ice as she stared at him. "Where is she?" She laughed, her voice a mixture of a witch's cackle and a depraved madman. "Oh, that is rich, Drake. You think I will just tell you without something in return? Apparently, you haven't thought this through."

Telsa rose to stand beside him. "How can you be so cold as to punish an innocent woman to snare a man who doesn't want you?"

Rose turned her icy stare toward Telsa. "When it comes to my life, I'll do anything. I will suck Maren's soul from her when Drake agrees to spend our lives together. That is the only way either of them will live. Drake with me, Maren forever trapped on the ship."

Drake grabbed her arm. "So she is on a ship. I don't care what you do to me, but you must return Maren."

Rose took a few steps back. "Let's discuss this over dinner.

I've prepared a lovely meal. No sense in it going to waste. Won't you enjoy your tea while I bring out the rest of the food?"

"If you think we'll eat anything you prepare, think again. I want answers, now. How do I find Maren?" he shouted.

"Is that a refusal, Drake? You won't agree to my terms?"

"I…I…"

Telsa grabbed his arm. "Don't do it, Drake. We'll think of something else. Please don't agree."

"I'm waiting," Rose said.

He studied Telsa's pleading eyes and felt the warmth of friendship. A trust had formed between them. He made his choice. "No, I do not agree to those terms. Too high a price. Besides, I don't trust you. If you need Maren's soul, then how can you set her free even if I do agree?"

"I will need Maren's soul. She will live, but forever on *The Lost Opal*. With Captain Nelson, of course."

"Nelson? There's someone else on the ship? You've done this before?"

Her laugh was deep and diabolical. "Oh yes, Drake, yes I have. My power is immense. I can do whatever I want."

"Not according to the Queen."

A glint of fear replaced the coldness in her gaze, and she shrugged. "A mere nuisance. She knows nothing of my power. I have her book of spells and have long studied how to keep my power should the worst come to pass." Her stance became defiant. "Do you agree or not?"

"No, I do not," he said.

"Then you leave me no choice." From her pocket she pulled a vibrating fire-red opal which took on an eerie glow in her outstretched hands. The room dimmed as if all the light transferred to the opal.

He felt its heat radiate, filling the room with a smoky acrid fog, which caused his nostrils to burn, and his throat to constrict.

Telsa dug her nails into his arm, coughing, her fear palpable. He clasped her hand willing their combined strength to stop whatever was about to come.

Rose's voice changed into something unrecognizable, a deep, raspy, guttural sound as she began to chant.

Hear this plea great stone of fire

And grant to me my soul's desire

The room disappeared as a whirlwind sucked him into its angry purple center.

Telsa lost her grip on his arm, and he heard her scream fade away into the darkness.

This man's heart for another grieves

Crushing my own until it bleeds

He was pulled upward, his body floating inside the twisting windstorm, consciousness leaving his body second by second.

Cast him now upon the waves

Sending him forever to the one he craves

Rational thought evaporated as he sped through the whirling vortex hearing only high-powered wind whoosh past his ears. Her chant faint now; he succumbed to the force that controlled him, and blackness rendered him unconscious as he floated away into nothingness.

CHAPTER EIGHTEEN

ROSE LISTENED TO THE WIND AS IT WHIRLED AROUND DRAKE and carried him away. An empty space, not unlike a black hole, replaced what once was a flesh and blood man.

Drake was gone.

For a moment, everything else receded from her mind. She'd banished her only chance for happiness. There was no time left to find another.

The opal's light faded. The stone was now simply a plain rock resting in her hand, cold and useless. She stuffed it in her pocket and turned her attention to Telsa who lay sprawled across the sofa, eyes wide and filled with terror.

"Well, now. What are we going to do with you?" She took a step toward her frightened guest and held out her hand. "Come, let's have our dinner. I have something special for you to taste. Just because Drake is gone doesn't mean we can't enjoy our evening. New friends and all that, you see."

Telsa pulled back from Rose's outstretched hand, and sputtered, "No, I…I must go." She dug in her purse for Drake's car keys.

"I'm afraid you're not going anywhere, my dear. I can't let you go after what you witnessed. Please eat with me. We'll decide your fate later."

Telsa ducked around Rose and sprinted toward the door. She fell hard against it, fumbling with the doorknob.

Rose reached for the fleeing woman, but stumbled, losing her balance. She caught herself before she lost all control, but not before Telsa bolted out of the door.

Dizziness prevented her from following. *What in tarnation is this about? I feel weak, as if the life is draining out of me.* She grabbed a chair and stood still, waiting for the vertigo to pass. The sound of the jeep's engine revving only made her angry. No way could she stop her now.

The heaviness of the inactive rock in her pocket revived her for an instant. She pulled it out and spoke aloud, "Stop her!"

There wasn't so much as a flicker. The opal was completely dead.

Fear struck her soul. She collapsed into the chair. "What's happening?" Breathing became labored; perspiration poured from her forehead and into her eyes.

Thirty minutes passed. She stood slowly, testing her footing. *Okay, a little strength has returned. I must rest to restore my power, and that of the stone. I let my anger overwhelm me; spent too much energy on Drake. A lesson for next time.*

She stumbled to the bedroom and fell limp across the bed. *Telsa will summon the police. I must be strong when they arrive.* The ability to think fled and she sank into a mind-numbing stupor.

How long did I sleep? She struggled to open her eyes and look at the clock. *Three a.m..*

Memory drifted back as she sat up, brushed her tangled hair away from her face, and concentrated on the queasiness roiling in her stomach. She swallowed hard, fighting to keep the bile at bay. *Why am I so sick?*

"Telsa!" she shouted to the empty room. "The cops haven't come. Maybe she didn't tell them what happened. I must find out what she did so I can plan my strategy."

She staggered to the bathroom, splashed cold water on her face, and hurried to the kitchen.

The meal sat untouched on the counter, ruined. *Can't bother about that now. I need to locate Telsa.* She pulled out the opal and held it in her palm. "Find Telsa."

There was no life in her magical rock. *It is useless. What is happening? Surely, I haven't lost it all.*

The coffee pot caught her eye. She shouted with glee, "Just the ticket. A stout cup will recharge my batteries."

A light rain pattered on the roof while the rejuvenating aroma of fresh coffee permeated the air. Strength flowed back into her body as she sipped the hot brew. Worried about her lack of power, she contemplated Drake's words when she answered his question, 'You've done this before?' She was cavalier in her reply, 'My power is immense. I can do whatever I want.' Smug in her confidence, he left her shaken when he countered with, 'Not according to the Queen.'

"The Queen," she whispered to the empty room. "Has she done her worst to me?" The opal was dead weight in her pocket, but she drew it out and looked at it with renewed intent. "Show me your light." To her astonishment a slight flicker sent a thrill through her. "It's coming back."

She set it on the table, stood back, and studied the stone. *Time, it needs time. And so do I. My power will come back.*

Extreme anger depleted her abilities; she understood that now. "I must be more careful in the future," she growled, "I need to concentrate on Telsa, at this point. Find out if she contacted the police."

The final gulp of the now lukewarm coffee rejuvenated her spirit as she announced to the room, "I'm not done yet."

Armed with a warm flannel shirt, sweats, a hooded raincoat, and oh yes, a carving knife in her pocket, Rose ventured out into the early morning darkness, destination Maren's place. Since her powers were compromised at the moment, the only recourse she had was to see for herself if Telsa was still there. The walk was slow going, the wet sand heavy, slowing her down. A flashlight did little to illuminate the black night, and she saw no other lights as she passed by each cabin. This was a perfect time to do some sleuthing.

She stopped short in front of Drake's cabin, dark and lonely now. *I wonder if Malcolm needs tending. I forgot about him when I lost control. I'll stop on my way back and take him to my house.*

As she shook off the reverie, she took a deep breath, and trudged on. *I messed up big time. Drake is gone, my last chance for a life out of the sea, and I haven't enough power to bring him back. I was stupid and selfish letting my anger get the best of me. My opal must return to its full strength because I am desperate now.*

Her thoughts rested on how she would secure a replacement for Drake. Telsa fit the bill as far as soul-taking, but the problem would be a new man. Most likely the first man who came her way would have to do. She was acquainted with a few on the beach. That red-headed boy, Josh came to mind. *He seems rather gullible. I assume he's still living here. He didn't have any sort of job that would take him away. Yes, it will have to be Josh.*

She neared Maren's cabin. Drake's jeep was parked beside Telsa's Acura SUV. She growled aloud when she saw the vehicles side by side. *So, the little minx had presence of mind to keep his jeep close by. I'll have to be crafty to overpower this one.*

Closer now, she didn't see any lights on. *Still asleep. That's good.*

She crept up behind Drake's vehicle and punched holes

in two of the tires with the knife she'd slipped into her pocket. Telsa's Acura suffered the same fate. *That will slow her down, give me a chance to subdue her.*

The sky lightened a bit giving her a sense of urgency. *Won't do to get caught in the daylight.* Her steps were soundless on the front deck. She peered through the living room window but didn't see any sign of life. *Should I knock, see if I can rouse her?* Second thoughts nixed that idea. *My powers aren't fully restored. That might be a mistake.*

She decided to peer into the other windows around the house, but as she carefully navigated the porch stairs, a deep growl sounded deep within the cabin. *Malcolm! She has Drake's dog.*

Fear gripped her. *I must leave. I don't have the power to fight both of them.*

She turned to go but stopped in her tracks at the sound of Telsa's voice and the bolt action of a rifle.

"Going somewhere, Rose?"

CHAPTER NINETEEN

T HE *LOST OPAL* SHUDDERED MUCH LIKE A SONIC BOOM rippling through the sky, the loud clap lasted only a second, but rattled everything on deck. The huge masts billowed and curled as if a strong wind blew through.

Maren was emerging from the galley on the way to her room when it hit. She white-knuckled the railing as she glanced up. *Baby blue, no clouds, not even a breeze.*

Captain Nelson clamored up the stairs behind her, white-faced, eyes wide. "What was that? Are we under attack?"

She let go of the rail and pulled him onto the deck. "No, sounded like a sonic boom. I've heard it many times. Odd it would happen out here."

"What in tarnation are you talking about?" He stared at her as if she had two heads.

She laughed, "I forget, you wouldn't know what that is given you lived a couple of centuries ago. It's a shock wave from an aircraft traveling faster than the speed of sound. Makes a loud bang. Happens frequently in my time."

His eyebrows knotted in consternation. "You mean a contraption flying about in the air? How in the blazes can… well, I don't even know what that means."

"There's no way I can make you understand the concept. It's common, however, where I live." She surveyed the deck.

"Something made the loud noise, but I don't see any damage caused by the vibration."

"Should we check the rest of…," he began.

Footsteps alerted them at the same time.

"Someone is here," they said in unison.

The captain unsheathed the dagger secured on his belt. "Might be Rose."

In the next instant, a disheveled man staggered around the rigging of the main mast and fell to his knees. "Help me," he said, the words barely audible.

She recognized the voice before she even saw his face. "Drake!"

They rushed forward and grabbed his arms just as he lost consciousness.

"You know him?" Nelson hoisted the man to his feet.

She struggled to drape his other arm around her neck. "Yes, he's Captain Drake Morgan. I've told you about him."

"Blow me down. Rose must be up to new tricks."

"Where shall we take him?"

Nelson indicated with his chin. "Your quarters are close. Let's take him there for now."

The young, disoriented captain moaned as they settled him on the bed. Black curls matted his sweating brow and drooped into both eyes as he tried to open them, with little success.

She soothed him and brushed his hair to the side. "Rest now, you need to sleep. You'll feel better if you just give in and let your body recuperate." His reaction to the time travel brought back the memory of her own experience. She shuddered.

He struggled once more to open his eyes, succeeding with only one. "Maren?"

"Yes, I'm here. I won't leave you. Sleep."

Her words appeared to pacify him as his body went limp and he receded into slumber.

"Looks like he's been through quite an ordeal. Much like you did when you first got here," said the captain.

"Time travel drains your strength. It'll be a few hours before he comes around. At least he landed on deck. I was dumped below in the darkness."

"So, he is the reason for the big boom? I never heard anything when you arrived."

"Well, I can't explain it. I'm sure it happened. You might have been asleep when she sent me here. Or maybe she expended more power with him." She examined the sleeping Captain Morgan's face as if to find answers there. "Why would she get rid of Drake? He's the man she wants to be with. He must have refused, and she got angry. I guess we'll find out when he wakes up."

The old captain moved toward the door. "Well, if you're gonna stay with him, lass, I'll go make us a hearty supper. He'll need to regain his strength, just like you did. By the time I have it prepared he'll be awake enough to eat."

After Nelson left, she continued to gaze at Drake's face wanting to ask more questions about why he ended up here—afraid of what this meant for all of them. *Sleep will claim him for hours, however. I'll have to wait.*

A moan escaped his lips every so often and he'd reach out his hand. She always clasped it tight to reassure him and he'd settle back into slumber. She took the opportunity to fix his face in her mind, press the strength of his hand into her memory, and run her hand through the curls tumbling around his face. *He's a handsome man, to be sure.*

An unexpected desire trickled through her along with a yearning to kiss those lips. She gently dropped his hand, stood, and went to the window. No clouds floated in the beautiful azure sky, the depth made it easy to lose oneself, and reflect on absolutely nothing. But her mind was in turmoil. Excitement because he's here, but sorry at the same time. *I wonder what his arrival means for us, and then there's poor Malcolm.*

Thirty minutes passed and another moan shook her from the reverie. She hurried to his side.

"Maren," his voice hardly more than a raspy growl.

She grasped his hand. "I'm here."

"Water," he croaked.

A pitcher always stood by the bed, and she grabbed it, poured it into her little clay cup, and put it to his mouth.

He sipped weakly, but she was pleased at the amount he was able to take. "Good, you can have more in a bit. Go back to sleep."

"No." His eyes opened. "I must tell you…"

"Time for that later. You need to rest," she answered.

He struggled to sit up. "No time. I must tell you. We're all in jeopardy."

She tried to push him back against the pillows, but he brushed her hands away, and in one motion sat up swinging his legs to the floor.

"There's nothing urgent at this very moment, Drake. If we are to fight Rose, you'll need your strength. Please lie back," she urged.

"No, you don't understand. Telsa is in danger, as well. I don't think we have much time. We could all be doomed." He stood; wobbly, but upright.

"Telsa? What do you mean? She's in Seattle. How can she be at risk?"

His hands sought hers as he faced her. "When you disappeared, she came down to the beach, but Rose worked some kind of magic on her, and she went back to the city. Anyway, the spell that compelled her to leave wore off and she returned yesterday, or today, or whatever the hell day it is."

Maren gasped, "She's there alone?"

"Not quite." He told her the circumstances which led them

to Rose's house. "When she sent me through the vortex Telsa didn't make the journey with me. She's by herself in that witch's clutches. We have to help her."

Tears welled in Maren's eyes. "My God, she's at her mercy. Can you walk good enough to navigate some stairs? Captain Nelson is preparing supper. We can fill him in while you eat. If we're to figure this out, we need you strong."

He nodded.

She led the way with his arm around her shoulders. By the time they arrived at the galley entrance, his balance had returned, but she insisted on holding on to him while he maneuvered the steps.

Captain Nelson glanced up from chopping onions, eyes watering, bushy eyebrows knit in consternation. "You're up already? I imagine you're famished. Supper will be ready in a jiffy."

"You're right, he's not rested enough, but he has news, and it won't wait." She pulled out a chair for him.

Nelson set down the knife and focused on the new arrival. "Sounds ominous. I'm listening."

"I'll tell you what he's told me. He can eat while I explain," Maren decided.

"Right," the old captain turned and dished up the goulash, tore off a piece of fresh-baked bread, and slid it in front of Drake. "Coffee?"

Morgan nodded and dove into the food.

"Here's what I know so far. My editor, Telsa, returned to the beach to find me. She met Drake. They agreed to work together. He told her of Rose's invitation to dinner and how he accepted to possibly find news of me. He convinced her to accompany him, and after much persuasion, she finally agreed. Rose was very unhappy at this intrusion, gave him an ultimatum to be with her, he refused. She sent him here, which leaves Telsa in Rose's hands. We've got to figure out how to help her."

"That bilge-sucking harlot. Hard tellin' what she'll do to poor Miss Telsa." He scratched his beard. "But what *can* we do? We're bound on this ship."

Drake scraped the last bite from his plate, gulped the rest of the coffee, and looked up. "I found out something. It might put us on the right track. The other night, she summoned the Queen of the Mermaids and asked her help in subduing me into compliance. The Queen refused, banned her from the mermaid pod. This is what I understand. Rose's powers will diminish to the point she will eventually be stuck on land and be as mortal as we are."

Maren and Captain Morgan exchanged glances.

"You mean, she might not be able to do anything bad to Telsa?"

"No way of knowing. I'm hoping that is the case," he said.

Nelson moved to the stove, grabbed the coffee pot, and poured Drake another cup.

"Thanks. I don't think we know each other, but you look familiar. I'm Drake Morgan."

The old captain reached out a hand. "Yes, I've heard much about you. Captain Nelson, here. Henry will do though."

The two men shook with vigor.

"Nelson? Hmm, I have a bunch of Nelsons in my ancestry. We'll have to compare notes. Could be we're related. But right now, we need to concentrate on getting off this boat and helping Telsa."

Maren spoke up, "When I arrived here, I actually thought he was you. But he's so much older. Here's a shocker. He's over two hundred years old. Been on this ship most all the time, since he was a young man."

Drake eyed the man holding the coffee pot. "I'm not gonna ask how that's possible. I'm sure Rose had something to do with it. Right now, I can't help but think of Telsa."

"I agree," Maren said. "Where to start to get you up to speed?"

Nelson replied, "How about the clue we've been looking for?"

"Yes. Before all this happened, we had a clambake on the beach. Rose attended and filled us in on the folklore about a mermaid who takes another's soul within her to capture the man she wants. Just for point of reference, Captain Nelson here is the first erstwhile victim. He scorned her. She punished him. And here we all are." She sipped her coffee and looked to Drake.

He nodded. "I get it so far. Go on."

She continued, "Well, we've been looking for the clue to get us out of here. No one has found it. I feel like it's in the chant she shared with us on the beach that night."

Morgan asked, "Do you remember it?"

"Not word for word but here's the short version." Her brows furled as she struggled with the memory.

'Beware the siren's song of the sea,

Something about a moth to flame.

A mistake will require a key.

I remember she said to 'restore the soul.'

Then she said something about freedom in her smile,

A twinkle in her eye.

Here it gets vague in my memory. Something about a portal key and guile, and untying fetters.

Don't look at the view, blah, blah, blah, something about a fall.

Then the end was a secret clue, in plain sight but hidden from all.'

It all rhymed of course, but I only heard it once. I didn't commit it to memory. I wish I had. Does any of it sound familiar to you?"

Drake answered slowly, "Only a couple of things stood out. Her smile and a twinkle in her eye."

Maren frowned at him. "Why does that stand out? We've combed this ship, gone through all his books hoping to find a clue, but have come up empty. Nothing here resembles a woman with a smile or a twinkle in her eye."

Drake smiled. "That's where you're wrong."

CHAPTER TWENTY

WHEN TELSA LEVELLED THE REMINGTON BOLT-ACTION rifle at Rose it took all her strength not to pull the trigger. Anger made her hands shake, but concern for Maren and Drake calmed her enough to regain control. She waited for an answer.

Rose stood still.

"I asked you a question," Telsa growled.

Slowly, Rose turned, a crimson flush colored her cheeks. "Uh, well, I was coming to apologize, but chickened out." A nervous laugh followed. "I don't know what came over me. I was so disappointed in Drake." She shrugged. "He made me angry."

"You can put the rifle down, now, Miss Telsa." A young, female officer stepped around the corner of the cabin, pointing a revolver at Rose. "We've got this."

She lowered the weapon.

Another cop, older, graying at the temples with a hefty girth, emerged from the opposite side; gun drawn.

Rose's brows furled with obvious annoyance. "What is this? Why are the police here?"

"I called them," Telsa said.

"But why? This little incident was between the two of us."

"Put your hands above your head," ordered the older officer. "Now."

She offered a sweet smile. "Certainly." One hand went into the air, the other slipped into her pocket.

"I said both hands!" He approached carefully.

Rose drew her hand out of the pocket grasping a stone, raising it to the sky. "Exactly what am I being charged with, officer?"

The female cop reached her first. "Murder."

She glanced at Telsa over her shoulder. "Mur…oh that's rich. I didn't kill anyone."

Telsa returned her gaze with steadfast resolve. "Then maybe you can explain exactly where Maren and Drake are."

The cop pulled one hand down and applied the cuff, but as she tried to obtain the other hand, Rose shouted. **"Turn me loose and help me leave."**

In an instant the officer was grasping thin air, the handcuffs dangling in her hand.

Rose was gone.

⇒✳←

Sunlight pierced the darkness as Rose woke up flat on her back in a grove of spruce trees, the smell of fresh earth in her nostrils. "Where am I?" she spoke aloud to a small, yellow-breasted bird perched on a tree limb above her head.

The tiny, feathered creature chirped and flew away.

She turned her head and spied the opal lying beside her open hand. *The stone worked, but I'm so weak.* Minutes passed before she could sit up. Her head spun, so she eased back down. *I must discern where I am.*

Spruce trees surrounded her, as well as evergreen fir and maple. The dawn revealed brush, brambles, and moss-covered rocks. She stood, which took every bit of her strength. A chipmunk chattered at her from a downed log, birds sang their morning songs, and the sun rose higher, giving much needed light and warmth.

The stone lay on the ground, dark, no more than a worthless rock. She picked it up. "You saved me from their clutches, but can you save me now?"

Her hand closed over the dysfunctional gem while she chanted softly, **"Reveal my location, I demand."**

Nothing.

She squeezed harder and repeated louder, **"Reveal my location, I demand."**

Still nothing.

I've used all its power. I'm stuck. How will I ever find my way out? She slipped the opal into her pocket.

Again, she took a quick survey of her surroundings. An animal trail led deeper into the trees. She kept her voice low, "Better not go that way. No telling what I'd run into."

An opening in the opposite direction looked promising. *I might find something through there.* Her steps were wobbly, but determination kept her going. After about a quarter of a mile, the grove parted, and the ocean came into view, but it was miles away. She was on a cliff.

The sheer edifice was too steep to climb down, so she turned back into the woods. Another quarter of a mile and she spied a rundown old shack. *Someone might be inside.*

The door stood ajar. She glanced around, cautiously. As she approached, a barking dog came around the corner of the cabin. He was shaggy and unkempt, but he kept his distance.

She froze, but said in a calm voice, "Hello boy. I'm a friend." She reached out a hand, but the canine stayed in protective mode and wouldn't approach. Under her breath she said, "Well, someone must be nearby if there's a dog."

"Who goes there?" a man called.

The pooch ran back to his master and together they

approached. The man was quite old, a long white beard matched scraggly, shoulder-length hair. He held a shot gun pointed directly at her.

"I'm lost. I hoped I'd find someone who could tell me where I am?"

"Lost? Well, how'd ya get here? This is private property, ya know. You're not welcome," the old codger said.

"Well… I… don't remember how I got here. I woke up in the trees back there."

"Hmmph. What? Were you kidnapped?"

"I really don't know. I don't seem to recall anything." That wasn't true, of course, but she dare not let on what actually happened.

"Well, I can't help you. Go back the way you came." He turned and started for the cabin door.

She pleaded, "Sir, if you would simply tell me where I am and how I can go back to civilization."

He stopped.

The dog growled.

He lowered the butt of the rifle to the ground and stood looking at her. "Lost ya say. Well, I suppose I can point you in the right direction."

"You wouldn't happen to have a cup of water would you?"

After a moment of hesitation, he gave a curt nod. "Come in the house. I'll give you water and a chunk of bread. It's all I can spare."

She hurried after him, saying thank you over and over.

"No need to thank me. I just want to be rid of you."

The cabin was in disarray. Dirty dishes on a rough-hewn sideboard. Torn, faded curtains. An unmade bed in the corner with a rumpled patchwork quilt done in red and blue, the only color in the room.

He pointed to a rickety chair beside a wooden table. "Sit yourself down. I'll get the water and the bread."

She sat down gently, wondering if the unsteady chair would hold her. "I'm ever so grateful."

He plunked a tin cup in front of her along with a chunk of bread. No butter. Just a dry crust.

The old man and the dog stood together watching her eat.

The water was warm, the bread almost impossible to chew, but she needed the sustenance and the time, so did her best, taking a bite, followed by a gulp of water.

When she finally choked the last of it down, she swallowed hard and spoke. "I don't know how to repay you for your kindness. I…"

"No need, no need. Come along and I'll point out the way for you."

She brushed the crumbs from her clothes and stood to follow him but stopped when she saw a shelf full of dried herbs. "Oh, you make your own spices?"

"They're not spices and it's none of your business."

Despite his rough tone, she decided to look them over and moved closer. "So, what are they, medicines?"

"You might say that." He gestured with his gun. "Move before I lose my patience."

She approached the shelf and touched each bottle. "I see bay leaf, cayenne, and this one looks like honey suckle." She also noted glass containers of small bones, one of feathers, another of fangs and claws. *Ingredients for certain spells. Reminds me of my own collection.*

"I said it is none of your business. Now move."

She stepped out into the sunshine with both man and dog behind her. "You've been so kind, I want to thank you, somehow. Could I clean up your dishes or straighten the cabin for you?"

"No. I don't need any help. You gotta go. Head through that

clearing in the trees. There's a town about five miles. Now, git on with ya."

Rose felt as if she'd struck gold. Those bottles were very familiar to her.

She turned to face him, and declared, "You're a wizard, aren't you?"

CHAPTER TWENTY-ONE

ALTHOUGH THE AFTERNOON HEAT TURNED THE GALLEY into a sauna, Maren's arms prickled with gooseflesh at Drake's statement.

She held his gaze. "We're wrong? But we've searched everywhere. There's no woman's smile or twinkling eye."

Drake nodded and said, "*Inside* the ship. But haven't you forgotten one thing?"

She and Captain Nelson exchanged glances.

"What have we missed?" Maren turned her attention back to Drake.

"The figurehead on the bow. It's a woman, I warrant, and I haven't even seen it yet."

Nelson relaxed his shoulders and laughed. "You don't think I've been on this ship for all these years and not thought of that? I've looked it over more times than I can count."

"Her eyes. Tell me about the eyes in the carving," Drake persisted.

The old captain stroked his beard. "Well…let me see. I don't recall. It's all wood, you know. Nothing special about the eyes."

"Are you sure? Have you experimented with the time of day, morning, or evening? The light catches those things at certain times, at different angles." Drake stood and brushed the hair from his brow. "I'd be willing to bet at the right time, when the light is just right, there'll be a sparkle of an opal in her eye. That's what the ship is called, right? *The Lost Opal.* The name caught my attention because I've always had a fascination with figureheads. Not sure where that came from." He paused a moment, looking into space, then continued. "Anyway, it's the first thing I thought of when I started to regain my faculties. And most important… Rose was wearing one around her neck when she sent me here."

Silence filled the room.

Drake might have something here. I should have thought of it myself.

Nelson's face lit up. "I never really questioned the name. You see, my assignment on this ship began when I was young. I'm actually the second captain to command *The Opal.* I was wrapped up in my first commission."

Maren bit her lip as she contemplated Drake's theory. *Can it be that simple?* "It's been right in front of us all the time. How could we be so blind? The name of the ship should have given us the obvious clue. The figurehead…it must be."

"I've stared at the thing many times over the years. Never once did it occur to me." He removed his cap and slapped his knee. "Well, blimey, let's not waste any more time."

Drake put up his hand. "Wait. The sun is going down. I assume there is only one time of day when you can see the glint in her eye. Could be sunset, but I feel it's more the morning sun. However, we can check it out. There's probably a very short window of opportunity. The three of us need to do this in shifts. Let's go scope it out."

Together they headed to the top deck.

Maren kept a close eye on Drake but was convinced his strength reached almost one hundred percent.

Captain Nelson reached the top of the stairs first.

When they all stood above deck, Maren took a deep breath. "My God, I hope we see the opal."

At the bow, she leaned over to take a good look at the figurehead, fearing disappointment, her heart pounded with anticipation. "There she is. How beautiful. I've looked at it before, but never really studied it." She edged farther over. "Wow, I did not realize it's a mermaid. Her tail is a beautiful deep blue."

Nelson pushed up next to her. "What about the eyes. Do you see anything?"

"No, it's all wood. No stone, at least on this side. We'll have to move to the left to see the other eye." She hurried to the other side, hoping to find a clue.

Drake was already there. "Nothing like a stone. Still looks like wood."

Exasperated, Maren sighed deeply and slapped the railing. "Shoot. Another dead end."

"Not necessarily. There's no light shining directly on it. We may have to wait 'til the sun hits it or the moon."

"But I don't understand what will happen if we find the opal. So it twinkles, then what?" Maren leaned over again to study the decorative piece.

Drake shrugged. "I imagine we'll have to see what happens when the light hits it. I'm not an expert in these things. Now we have three heads working on it and have a better chance to figure things out. Can't hurt to try. You've been here a while Maren, and still no solution."

A defensive reaction caused her to spit out the words, "You think I haven't tried? I don't want to be here anymore than you do, Drake."

"Whoa, Maren. I get it, no need to bite my head off. Like I said, we'll all look at this from different angles. We'll figure it out."

"Sorry. I'm just so frustrated."

The sun reached the horizon and sank slowly into the ocean. No light glinted from the eyes of the figurehead.

Maren frowned. "I must say, I'm disappointed."

Drake put his hand on her shoulder. "There's still the moon and the morning sun. Who takes moon watch?"

Nelson spoke first. "I will."

Maren shook her head. "No, Captain, you should rest. After all, you're the cook around here. Drake, you need sleep to fully recover. I'll take it."

Captain Nelson spoke first. "Agreed. I'll go straighten up the galley. You two figure out your sleeping arrangements."

The sun dipped below the horizon in a hurry, leaving a black sky in its wake while the stars took their time making an entrance.

Her body tingled when Drake's arm brushed hers as darkness descended. She couldn't believe he was standing right next to her. Another ripple of her flesh caused her heart to skip a beat when he spoke in that deep, mellow tone.

"Ah yes, sleeping arrangements. I take it the room I recovered in is not the room I will occupy permanently?"

A blush warmed her cheeks at the thought of him in her bed, thankful the dusky sky hid the transparency on her face. "Well, no. That's my room. It was the most convenient when we found you. There's another cabin just around the corner, smaller, but adequate. Come on, I'll show you."

He followed without a word.

I wonder what he's thinking. I imagine nothing like the scenes dancing in my head.

"Here we are." She opened the door. "It's clean. Has all you'll need. I suggest you get some sleep while you can. I'll be on deck watching for the moon." She turned to go.

"Wait." He touched her arm. "Thank you for taking such good care of me. The journey here was quite harrowing, but I'll recover. It helps to know I found you. I can't think of anyone else I'd rather be stranded with than you."

Her breath caught and then she whispered, "I'm so happy

to be here for you, Drake. You helped me when I needed it. I'm glad to return the favor."

"It's more than that, Maren. The night I met you on the beach.…you had a look about you I can't explain. Innocent, but strong. Feisty, but vulnerable. You were so beautiful, dressed in that skimpy night dress. I remember the soft shade of pink. I haven't been able to get you out of my mind."

"I…I better get out on deck. The moon is probably out by now." She fled before the urge to kiss him overwhelmed her.

The sky was dark, masked by clouds, hiding the stars. She flung herself against the railing and tried to slow her breathing. The moon peeked out for a moment, high in the sky, shining like a beacon. The conversation with Drake receded as she focused on the figurehead. The light did not illuminate the wooden mermaid. She struggled to see the eyes, willing the ivory, celestial orb to reveal an opal within the gaze of the aquatic sprite.

But it didn't.

She ran from side to side, studying the eyes, hoping for some sign, losing hope as the night dragged on. Three hours passed; the moon was at its peak with no hidden secret unveiled.

Dark clouds gathered across the sky. *There'll be a storm in a few hours. I can smell the rain. The moon is hidden now, no more chances for it to work its magic on the mermaid.*

Lack of sleep made it difficult to keep her eyes open and she lay her head down on the railing, wishing for morning.

"Why don't you get some shut eye."

Drake's voice made her jump. She rubbed her eyes, smoothed her tousled hair, and dared a glance into his dark eyes. The lantern hanging on a hook-like sconce next to her gave off just enough light to see the twinkle reflecting the flame. "I just need some coffee that's all. I'll make it 'til morning. You should be sleeping."

"Can't sleep. Toss and turn. I keep thinking about you."

A silence rose between them.

The moon appeared, drifting out from the clouds, bathing Drake and herself in an astral light while the waves slapped against the ship beating out a soft rhythm, filling the air with the sound of the ocean's music.

He leaned forward.

The atmosphere charged her body with desire; electricity so intense she found it hard to keep a level head. "Drake, don't, please. We must concentrate on Telsa's…"

He didn't listen.

Before she could protest, his arms wound around her and his lips pressed hard, yearning, full of need. The strength to pull away deserted her and she gave in to his hungry fervor, melting into him, devouring his mouth, feeling his muscular arms engulf her even tighter.

Finally, they pulled apart at the same time.

Yearning made it hard to breathe, and words would not come.

He gazed deep into her eyes. "I've been wanting to do that for a very long time."

CHAPTER TWENTY-TWO

ROSE WATCHED THE OLD MAN START AT THE SUGGESTION OF his wizardry, which gave credence to her statement.

He didn't answer but shot her a killer look.

Hands on her hips, chin in the air, she stated defiantly, "Well, I'm waiting."

He raised the shotgun and pointed directly at her. "Ye best be leavin' my property if ya know what's good for you."

She stood her ground. "I'm not leaving until you answer me. I'm a wizard in my own right. A mermaid if you will. Outcast and alone, but a mermaid, none the less." Her voice softened using her most sympathetic tone. She went on. "I need your help."

For a moment, he didn't move, continued to study her as he slowly lowered his weapon. "What sort of help?"

An inward sigh relaxed her body. "Your potions. I need assistance in concocting one to send me back to where I came from and restore my power." She reached into her pocket and withdrew the stone. "This opal is the only thing I have left to work with, but its power is diminished leaving me stranded. I can't wait on the opal; I must go back."

"Why are you an outcast from your people? I can't help you if you are some kind of outlaw. Wizards come from all over for my services. That's why I live way out here, to be left alone." He hesitated. "But you are here at present, so give me your story."

The sun was high in the sky now, so bright she had to squint to keep him in focus. Warm perspiration trickled down her back as she pleaded with him. "Can we go inside? The sun…well, I'm tired and need to sit down."

At first he just stared at her, but eventually turned toward the cabin. "Alright, follow me. I'll give you one shot."

Inside, he set the shotgun down by the fireplace and motioned for her to sit at the table.

He poured her another cup of water, slid it across the table to her, and sat down.

After a quick sip, she relayed the story—her banishment and waking up in this place.

He remained quiet as she talked, engaging her eyes as if to ferret out any lies. When she finished he sat quietly, gaze still trained on her.

"Aren't you going to say anything?"

"That's quite a tale—if I believe you. I don't cotton to your kind especially. Don't think I have anything that can help you." He stood and gestured toward the door; his manner dismissive.

"Oh, but I think you do. May I look at your supplies?"

A sigh of impatience deflated his body. "I guess that can't hurt. Mind you don't touch anything."

She stood and went to the shelves. "What kind of wizard are you? Where do you hail from?"

"I've been around for a hundred years. Came over from England where they threatened to do me harm if I didn't mend my ways. Been holed up here for quite a spell. Keep to myself. Don't want no trouble."

"I mean you no harm." She smiled. "What do they call you?"

"Nox, if you insist. Better yet, don't call me anything, just forget you ever saw me."

"Ah," she said. "Nox means *night* in Latin. Are you some kind of dark prince?"

"Don't like to talk about it, but your knowledge of Latin intrigues me. I've never known a mermaid. Wasn't sure they had any book smarts. Guess I'm wrong."

She examined the bottles. "There's a lot I could tell you about our kind, but maybe another time. I think you have what I need." After pulling a few off the shelf, she turned to him. "May I concoct a potion?"

A frown wrinkled his old forehead as he watched her pull some bottles off the shelf. "Well…how long will it take? I told you not to touch anything. I don't want you hangin' around. You need to go."

"Just long enough to brew this tea and deliver me back to where I came from." She carried the items to the stove. "Do you have a container? I must warm the brew on the stove."

He pulled one from the overhanging pots. "Well make it snappy. Remember you cannot under any circumstances reveal my whereabouts. I only want to be left alone."

"Certainly." She took the beat-up saucepan and added the ingredients. A pinch of this, a dab of that, a little stir, and a cup of water finished off the concoction.

He eyed her carefully, guarding his precious bottles. The room filled with the aroma of rosemary.

"Almost done."

After the brew simmered a bit, she pulled the pot from the heat and stirred.

"I'll need you to say an incantation for the spell to work properly."

He eyed her with distrust. "How do I know you won't trick me?"

"My dear Nox, I do not want to cause you harm. I want to leave here as much as you want me gone."

"Fine. What's the incantation?"

"Are you familiar with the travel spell? Sending people to other places?"

"Yep, used it multiple times."

"Okay, while I drink this brew, you can say the incantation." She poured the tea into a tin cup and sipped.

He scratched his head, but began, **"From whence this person travelled, send her back henceforth."**

They waited.

The spell should have worked immediately, but she still stood in the cabin with the old wizard looking at her, distrust in his gaze.

"Are you playin' with me? Did you make a mistake? You should be gone."

"I don't understand what happened. And I'm sure the ingredients are right. I've done this a hundred times. Maybe it's me. My powers have been stripped."

He scratched his head as he eagle-eyed her. "You say your powers were stripped. Might make the spell invalid."

"That shouldn't matter. I'm the one you are sending away. My powers or a lack thereof should have no bearing." She took another sip of the tea. "Say it again."

He repeated the spell. Still nothing happened.

"Might be that you need to drink it, too.

"Mebbe." He poured a cup and took a swig and said the incantation again.

Nothing happened.

"Well, we have a conundrum. Something is blocking your exit. Let me see that stone."

She offered it to his outstretched hand.

After examining the opal, he handed it back to her.

"Seems to me, this stone is blocking your way. I think in order for the spell to work, the stone needs to be in full power."

She reacted like a deflated balloon and sat down at the table. "But that will take almost twenty-four hours. What will I do in the meantime? I must get home."

He pulled the chair out and thumped the flat of his hand on the table's surface. "Blazes be. I can't have you hangin' around for that long."

Tears moistened her eyes; she wiped them away with a frustrated swipe. Millenia had passed since she felt the sting that now blurred her vision. The hackles of her heart had hardened over the years. She refused to allow the emotion to govern her. But now, the realization of her action toward Drake and Maren sparked a niggle in the depths of her soul. *Could I be feeling remorse?*

They sat in silence for a few minutes.

Nox snapped his fingers. "I might have a solution. Come with me." He grabbed his rifle, clucked at the dog to follow, and made his way out of the door.

Hopeful, she stood and followed him.

He stopped by an old Juniper tree, knotted, and twisted after years of standing high on this mountain, unseen by anyone but old Nox. "Stand over here, under the lower branch."

She did as instructed. "How can this help?"

Nox positioned himself just out of reach of the tree and had his dog lay even farther away. "You just wait and learn. This old tree is over a hundred years old. Planted the sprig myself. Came from the old country. My grandmam, a witch, trusted me with her prized possession." He beamed at this revelation. "Said it has magical powers. I've never had reason to test the tree before, so we'll see what happens."

He plucked a leaf from the lower branch, held it in the palm of his hand, and whispered the spell.

She strained to hear the words but couldn't. The sky darkened, a subtle rumble reached her ears, and lightening danced across the heavens.

And then poof! She fell into a black hole, tumbling through time and space.

CHAPTER TWENTY-THREE

MAREN, RELUCTANT TO WITHDRAW FROM THE PASSIONATE kiss or the intense embrace, gazed at Drake while emotions bounced inside her body like tumbleweeds across an open desert. The words came out reluctantly. "Drake, this isn't the time or place. We need to find the opal."

The electricity faded instantly.

His shoulders sagged.

He took a deep breath. "You're right, of course. I'm sorry. I've had this pent up inside me ever since we met. Telsa's reappearance only intensified my urgency to find you." He scanned the bright blue sky as the golden sun made its entrance upon the day. "I'm guessing you didn't find anything. No glint off the mermaid's eyes? Nothing?"

She stepped farther away from him and released his hand. "No, I've run back and forth trying to spot any sign of the gem, but sadly, it's been a waste of time. So, what do we do next?"

As he opened his mouth to answer, Captain Nelson sprinted from the galley.

"Breakfast is ready." Nelson's face, red from the heat of the stove and dotted with drops of perspiration, nevertheless revealed a happy countenance. His breath came in quick huffs as he ascended the stairs. A cup of coffee sloshed in his left hand which he pushed toward Maren.

She took the warm mug, grateful for the distraction, and addressed the men, "You two go down to breakfast. I'm gonna wait a bit, see if the morning sun reveals anything."

Her gaze rested on Drake, and she became lost in his eyes. She saw the longing, and a primal need to kiss him again welled, but she resisted.

His gaze searched hers for a few seconds more.

The electricity between them intensified until she was sure he would abandon everything and kiss her right in front of the old captain.

Instead, he rubbed the stubble on his chin, and said, "I need a shave. I'll join you after I freshen up."

Captain Morgan's face blotched a purple hue as he ran one hand across his face. "Well, it won't stay hot for long, so don't dally." He hurried back down the stairs to the galley.

Drake said nothing more, just turned and walked briskly toward his cabin.

She watched him, his muscular back broad and strong, his virility evident in his youthful stride, then hastily turned toward the sea and sipped the coffee letting the ocean waves soothe her soul.

Drake shut the door to his small, but serviceable room, and noted the single bed and the one drawer night table. He shook off the tiredness and dismissed the indulgence of a short nap. A cherrywood shaving mirror atop a tall ornate stand stood like a sentry in front of the window. All the tools he needed lay in perfect order, ready for use. *I sure need a shave.*

He stripped off his shirt and studied his reflection in the oval mirror. While he mixed the lather, he continued to stare into its silvery depths. Something drew him in.

And then he saw it—a spark of light from within the glass.

He leaned in to examine the phenomenon closer. A quick glance around the room didn't reveal the source of the light, so he returned his attention to the mirror. Just as the clouds moved across the sky, the golden sun's aura beamed through the window and activated the shaft of light shooting from the mirror. *The sun and the mirror. I was right about the light, just not the vehicle. We've been looking in the wrong place.* The urge to shout out to the others disappeared as the glow waned, then went out altogether. *I should wait until I'm sure about this. After all, I arrived here bearing hope. I proved off base with the mermaid theory. I can't keep building their hopes only to dash them over and over.*

After he finished shaving, he pulled on a clean shirt from the closet and studied his reflection again. The window darkened. *Maybe when the sun peeks out again, the shaft of light will show.*

He concentrated on the sky and waited.

A slight breeze moved the clouds along and, once again a bright bar of light shot from the mirror, but only for a moment. He ran his finger over the spot on the glass. Sure enough. *Something is embedded within the glass.*

After a studious examination, he decided it was indeed an opal; tiny, but nonetheless there. *I must be positive. I'll wait until this next group of clouds moves through to be sure.*

He ran his thumb over the glass again. The divot, subtle, but there, completely disappeared when the sun no longer connected to the mirror. *Okay, I've proved it to myself, now I have to convince the other two. What do we do with it? Can it help us get out of here?*

As a former captain, he understood the importance of leading with authority and calmness. He finished his morning grooming and decided to enjoy a hearty breakfast before he broke the news.

⊷⊱⊰⊶

Maren glanced up as Drake skipped down the galley stairs to join them. Her breath caught when she noticed his freshly shaved face and his rambunctious black curls now tamed. The fresh chambray shirt made his blue eyes pop.

The kiss they'd shared brought a rush of heat to her face.

Captain Nelson turned to greet him in his usual brisk way. "Took your time, aye mate? Maren here has about whisked up everything."

"I have not! There's plenty."

The old captain's belly jiggled with his silent laughter.

Drake pulled out a chair and settled beside her. "Sorry I came late. Took my time. A good shave helps wake me up."

Nelson pushed a plate of hotcakes and a pot of maple syrup toward him, along with a steaming cup of coffee.

Drake tried to say thank you, but with a mouthful of the fluffy cakes he could only nod his appreciation.

She examined his face as he scarfed down his breakfast. *I see a glow in his eyes. Wonder if he's up to something.*

Unable to keep her thoughts to herself, she asked, "What do you have up your sleeve, Drake? You look like a shark with a seal in its sites."

He raised his fork for another bite but stopped in mid-air. "Am I that transparent?"

Nelson chimed in, "Ye are, matey. Stop lollygagging. Out with it."

Drake continued to hold the fork aloft, gulped the last of the coffee, and said quietly, "I think I've found the opal." He shoved the bite into his mouth.

She didn't speak, couldn't, only stared at him.

The old captain spoke first. "And how did you come to find this thing?"

"Shaving," he said.

Maren stood; the chair tumbled over with the force. "I've been here for ages trying to solve this riddle. My patience is at an end. How can you sit there and be so nonchalant?"

He smiled. "Because I'm hungry?"

CHAPTER TWENTY-FOUR

NAUSEA ENVELOPED ROSE AS SHE TUMBLED uncontrollably inside the sinister black hole. Something wasn't right. She shouldn't be bumping back and forth, hitting the vaporous enclosure, losing all sense of balance. Granted, she'd never actually used this mode of travel, but from all accounts, this level of violence was unprecedented.

A scream rose to her throat, but the violent wind prevented its escape. Even her thoughts were jumbled, but she fought to stay coherent. *Why am I still conscious? I should have blacked out and awakened at my new destination, hopefully the beach, and that's only if Nox knew what he was doing.*

Her body changed from rolling to flipping head over heels, end over end.

She moaned, fighting the ever-present queasiness.

The trip went on forever, but finally she slammed into a hard surface expelling the breath from her lungs. A whiplash effect forced her head to hit the floor.

She passed out.

The passage of time didn't register as she eventually awoke, head throbbing, completely engulfed in a stuffy blackness with no way to know how long she'd lain there. *This isn't the beach. Did old Nox pull a trick on me? Or did he simply utter the wrong spell?* She scrambled to her feet, feeling her way in the darkness, touching walls which indicated a room of sorts. *But where?* Her toe rammed something solid, she shouted into the blackness. "Dang." She hopped up and down holding the offended appendage. When the pain subsided, she explored the area more thoroughly. *A step, and more than one. The stairway leads up. I'm in a basement or something.*

The floor heaved without warning, jerking her into the railing. The sound of water slamming into the outer wall alarmed her. A larger swell almost sent her backward. "A ship. I'm on a ship!"

Her eyes eventually adjusted to the darkness, but the blackness didn't reveal any source of light. Desperate to secure her freedom from the pit below deck, she followed the rickety rail until a door stopped her progress. Giddy with hope she groped the doorknob, pounded on the wooden barrier, but to no avail. No one came to her rescue.

A slice of fear sped down her spine. The comforting weight of the stone in her pocket no longer existed. She jammed a fist into one pocket. *I had it on me. It's got to be here.*

Empty.

The opal's power should be restored by now. I need it to open that door.

Slowly she slid her hand into the other pocket.

Nothing.

Frantic, she stumbled back down the stairs and fell to her knees running her hands over every inch of the floorspace. *The opal must have fallen out of my pocket. But where?*

No matter how thoroughly she searched, the stone simply was not there.

Could I have lost it in transport? I tumbled around pretty violently. If that's the case, my power may be gone forever.

She sat back on her heels in the murky gloom and covered her face with both hands, crying out loud. "I'm locked below deck in some ship and my power is non-existent. What am I to do?"

Captain Nelson trailed the other two as they clamored up the galley steps to take a look at the opal Drake supposedly found. He wasn't as nimble as they, so lagged behind.

The ship listed ever so slightly responding to a larger than normal swell. He gave himself a minute to steady his legs.

As the ship righted itself, something rolled across the deck floor. The object made a bumping sound as it travelled, then stopped at his feet.

He studied the thing, then picked it up. "What the…? Why I think it's a precious stone of some sort, but it looks raw, unpolished." As he turned it over in his hand, the unknown substance glowed slightly, shooting shards of light from deep within. As the light flickered, the illumination disclosed the identity of the stone. "An opal," he whispered. "My God, this is her opal. She's here."

Blood pumped in his ears as he glanced around the deck but saw no sign of Rose. He stuffed the opal in his pocket and headed toward Drake's quarters. *They mustn't know about this quite yet. I have to find her first and figure out what she's up to. No sense in scaring the bejesus out of them. She's without her opal which means she might be defenseless.*

Drake and Maren, heads together, studied the shaving mirror.

She looked up as the old captain entered. "Did you get lost on the way?"

Nelson chuckled, his belly jiggling with the effort. "No, I'm not quite as spry as you two. Takes me a minute." He came up behind them and peered into the mirror. "Find something?"

Drake turned to him. "Possibly. The light isn't right, but I showed Maren the slight indentation where the stone is embedded. Would you like to feel it?"

"Certainly. Show me."

Drake ran his finger over the spot.

The old captain followed Drake's lead. "There's something there all right, just barely. You say you saw the stone when the light hit at a certain time?"

"That's right. Saw it plain as day. An opal in all its splendor." Drake moved away so Nelson could look closer.

"What do we do, sit, and watch it? Then what? It's of no use if we don't know how to use it." He turned to Maren. "Any ideas?"

Maren frowned. "If only we had that spell book."

"What spell book? You never mentioned a book before."

She explained the *Book of Spells* she'd found in Captain Nelson's library, how they studied it, the strange appearance of Rose in her dream, and Nelson's banishment to the hold.

"Okay, then where is this book? We need it," Drake said.

"She took it," she stated flatly.

"Then how will we know how to use this thing?" he asked.

Captain Nelson slipped one hand into his pocket. Reassured the stone still nestled there, he said, "We need to start with my library again. Maybe the book returned on its own."

"Highly unlikely, since Rose is the one who took it," she said. "But Drake and I will start there. There's an answer somewhere on this ship. Rose is very devious. She's probably hidden some sort of clue in plain sight. Maybe not the book, but something. I suggest we start searching."

"What about the opal in the mirror? Is there a chance it might illuminate again? Shouldn't someone stay here to watch?" Nelson asked.

Drake shook his head. "The window is short for the sun to catch the opal, so tomorrow morning will be the best time. The only other opportunity might be the moon. I suggest we search the ship for the spell book. We can stand watch tonight when the moon comes out."

I have to examine the rooms below decks before I tell them Rose might be on board. "Sounds good. Two heads are better than one, so you two search the library. I'll go below and scope out things down there. Agreed?"

Maren nodded. "Let's go."

As his two compatriots left to search the library, he headed for the deck well leading to the rooms below. Most of the doors were closed, only a few stood open. He searched those first, to no avail. As he approached the last closed door, he thought he heard a sound.

What is that?

He stopped and listened. *Yes. Sounds like a woman crying.*

Sobs continued as he pressed his ear to the door. He tapped lightly. "Rose?"

Immediately, the crying ceased.

He tapped again. "Rose? Is that you?"

A moment passed.

A weak female voice answered, "Captain Nelson?"

"Yes, what are you doing here, Rose? How did you get locked in there?"

"Please help me," she pleaded. "A wicked wizard took his anger out on me and sent me here. I've lost my power. Get me out of here and I'll explain everything."

"Not a chance. I'm not falling for your lies or your tricks. I haven't spent over two hundred years on this ship without learning something from your wicked ways." He grasped the stone, which radiated a small amount of heat this time. "I'll be back when I've informed the others. Meanwhile, enjoy your stay."

Now I can tell them. Together we'll decide what to do with her.

CHAPTER TWENTY-FIVE

MAREN SEARCHED THE LOWER BOOKSHELVES WHILE Drake took the top, neither making any headway.

He stood on a small step ladder beside her, the closeness of his body hitting every sensory trigger. The kiss, the smell of his shaving cream, those darn curls. *Crap, at this point I hope we don't find the spell book and stay on this ship forever. But, of course, I'm being ridiculous. Telsa needs our help. We have to rescue her from Rose.*

His voice, baritone and smooth as honey, seeped into her thoughts. "What did you say, Drake?"

He climbed down the ladder, took her by the shoulders, and kissed her deeply. His hands remained on her shoulders as he pulled away. "I said I was having no luck finding the book."

She blinked, unable to catch her breath.

"I kissed you because your eyes glazed over, and your hand hasn't moved off that old journal for more than a minute. You were thinking of the kiss we shared on deck before, weren't you?"

She nodded, still speechless.

"So was I. The spell needed to be broken if we're going to find the book." He chuckled. "Did my tactic work?" He let go but held his hands out as if to catch her.

Her breath released. "I'm sorry," she spoke softly. "I don't know what came over me. I'm fine now, let's keep looking." She turned back to the shelf.

"Wait a minute. We can't deny our attraction for one another. Remember we're both feeling this. Don't run from the chemistry. At the same time, we need to focus on finding a way off this ship, but let's not push our desires down so far they disappear. Deal? I want you, Maren, and by the look on your face, you want me, too. If we acknowledge the emotion we can relax when we're around each other. Okay?"

She wasn't a flirt. Actually, quite the opposite. Her ability to focus on her job and resist male company was infamous. Her friends teased her incessantly. Said she'd end up an old maid. So, what happened next took her by surprise.

Her lips drooped into a frown, she lowered her eyes and took his hands. "I'm not sure this is real, Drake. Kiss me again."

The vibration from his throaty laugh reached their hands. He let go, wrapped his arms around her, and pressed a deep kiss on her all too willing mouth.

The clearing of an intruder's throat made them jump apart.

"Well, well. I see we are hard at work looking for the book," Captain Nelson laughed.

"I…we," she stammered.

Nelson waved a hand at her attempted speech. "No need to explain. Even a blind person can sense the chemistry between you two. I'm just sorry I had to interrupt. I have some news."

Drake released the embrace and turned to face the old man. "Good or bad?"

"Depends." He drew the opal from his pocket and presented it to them, hand outstretched." I found this on the deck and the owner is below locked in a room."

She blinked. "Looks like some kind of rock."

Drake spoke up, "I know exactly what that is. Rose used it to send me here."

"That's right. This stone is her opal," said Nelson.

"Is Rose the person below deck?" Drake asked.

"Yes."

Speechless, she trembled at the implications of Rose's presence. Instinctively, she grabbed for Drake's hand.

Drake continued his questions, "She'd never willingly give the opal to you. How did you take it from her? And how did you lock her up?"

"The stone rolled to my feet when that last big swell hit. At first I didn't recognize the opal until the thing glowed. I figured she was here somewhere and decided to find her before I told you. I found her in a locked room below deck, without her stone, and as far as I can tell, she has no other power, right now. I heard her crying."

Panic struck her. "We can't let her out. No telling what evil she'd do to us. Throw the stone into the sea."

Nelson shook his head. "Hold on now. This opal is our best chance to leave this ship. If we can find the book, we might find the right spell."

"But what if she figures a way out of the room? She'll come for us, do us harm, even kill us." She gripped Drake's hand tighter.

Drake took up the argument. "We can't let her out under any circumstances. We keep searching and leave her below deck." He looked at both of them. "Agreed?"

"She needs food and water. Can we be so cruel as to deny her? She did supply me with the essential amenities all these years," Nelson continued.

She held up a hand. "Wait. There might be a faster way to secure our freedom."

"Well, spill it. What?" Drake asked.

"The mermaids," she said.

Captain Nelson's eyes glowed with a new light. "Say, mate. You might have an idea there. Can we summon them?"

"We can try," she said.

"What are you talking about? Summon the mermaids?"

She recounted the story of the mermaid visit after her arrival. "The Queen gave a chant that would free us, but we haven't found Zeus's eye yet."

"The teardrop? Of course. In the mirror. The stone is shaped like a teardrop. What else can you remember about the chant?"

Nelson spoke up, "We wrote it down. Moonbeam was in the chant. I bet we watch for the moonlight to hit. You were right Drake. If not the sun, then the moon."

She let go of Drake's hand. "I left it in my room. Hold on."

A few minutes passed, but she returned with paper in hand. "Here goes,

If from this curse you will be free
A moonbeam will reveal the key.
Your hands on the portal must be
and repeat this mantra aloud times three.

As Cecella disappeared into the sea, she said,
"In plain sight the key resides.
A precious tear from Zeus's eye."

"Everything makes sense. What are we waiting for?" Drake pulled her toward the door.

Nelson stepped in front of them. "No. Not yet. We need to contact the mermaid Queen. We can't afford to mess this up. Rose might find a way out of that room and stop us, or she might stay in there forever. I don't want to leave it to chance. The Queen will know what to do."

She chimed in, "I agree."

"So, how do we contact her?"

"Let's go on deck. Maybe we can simply call out?" She led the way.

They scrambled outside and lined up along the railing.

"Maren, she's a woman. More than likely she'd respond to your call," Nelson suggested.

"Okay, here goes." She cleared her throat. "Queen Cecella, we need your help. If you hear us, please show yourself. It's a matter of life and death."

They waited.

Nothing.

"Try again," Drake urged.

"Oh, powerful Queen Cecella, leader of the mermaids, we beseech you to come to our aid."

"Listen!" Nelson said. "The musical voices of the mermaids. I'll never forget the sound."

The sing-song melody became louder, and in the distance, a haze hovered on the horizon. As the phenomenon moved toward them, they saw the outline of the beautiful creatures clearer, until they arrived just beyond the ship.

As before, the waters parted, and Queen Cecella appeared from the depths. "Your call reached me. You need my assistance?"

"Yes, oh Queen. You see, we found Zeus's teardrop. But now there are three of us, courtesy of Rose. She is locked below without her opal, with no power whatsoever, we think. Our concern is using the chant you gave us and only one or two of us make the transition. And of course, there's Rose. The dilemma to leave her there or free her. Captain Nelson is of the mind she needs food and water, as she provided for us those essential needs. Please guide us."

The Queen smiled. "I am pleased you have compassion for one who wronged you so despicably. It shows true character. I will help you."

Nelson spoke up, "Madam Queen, one more matter, please."

He held out the lightly charged opal. "I found this. She was separated from the stone and has no power."

Cecella nodded. "You are in possession of the two powers that will send you home. An important element for you. All you need to do is stand in front of Zeus's tear while holding the larger opal. Link your arms tightly. The ones on each end will touch the teardrop at the same time. Your arms must be linked. You will be transported back to your time immediately. No chant is necessary."

"No moonbeam?"

"No. The beam is how you found the opal. The amulet did its job."

"But the large opal isn't fully charged yet," Nelson said.

"It does not matter. As soon as you form the circle and touch the teardrop, the larger stone will be fully charged," the Queen explained.

Nelson frowned. "What of Rose?"

"As soon as you are transported, I will free her from the room. However, she will remain on the ship for the rest of her days."

"So, we can go now, this minute?" Drake asked.

"You may," said Cecella.

"Will you stay until we depart, Queen Cecella?" she asked.

"I will."

They hurried to the room with the mirror. Once inside, they put Captain Nelson in the middle while Drake and Maren stood on each end.

Nelson held the larger stone.

"Are we ready?" Drake looked at his partners.

"Wait," Nelson stopped them. "We didn't ask her what happens to me. But I don't care. I want to be off this ship. Live or die. So, if I disappear, you know I'm gone. You two be happy, stay together, love one another."

She whispered, "Are you sure?"

He nodded.

Drake took over. "Okay, on the count of three. You have a firm grip on the Opal?"

Nelson nodded again.

"One, two…"

The door burst open, and Rose stood, wild-eyed, hair disheveled. "No!"

"Three," Drake shouted.

CHAPTER TWENTY-SIX

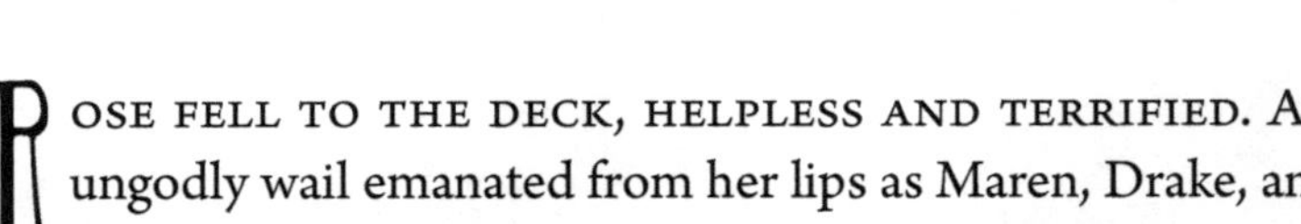

Rose fell to the deck, helpless and terrified. An ungodly wail emanated from her lips as Maren, Drake, and Captain Nelson disappeared into a kaleidoscope of light. She buried her face in both hands and sobbed. "My only chance to escape. I'm doomed forever."

"I am afraid you're correct, Rose. There is no way off this prison of your making."

The sound of Queen Cecella's voice made her scramble upright and then fall prostrate in front of the female sovereign (something she would never do if she weren't in a weakened state). "My Queen, I beg you, please don't leave me here. I am sorry for the cruel things I did. I offer my sincere remorse."

Cecella stood in the doorway enveloped in a gossamer gown, the delicate material moving with the wind, created an ethereal image. The crystal crown sparkled atop her head, twinkling with the gems of the ocean. "The crimes you committed were judged by the council. They agree. You will remain here with no recourse to salvage any kind of life other than on this ship."

Rose's pride always kept her strong and defiant, able to withstand the fiercest situations, but this time the cold hand of fear squeezed tightly. Tears streamed hearing the Queen's edict. "You can't do this. I said I was sorry. I only wanted to be happy, live on land, out of the sea. I didn't do anything so bad, did I?"

The Queen stepped aside and pointed to the open deck. "See for yourself the destruction your actions wreaked."

Rose took a step past the sovereign and witnessed the one thing she'd never considered before. The ghosts of all the women whose souls she took over the years. All who drowned themselves in their agony.

They shouted, pointed, and condemned her.

"Evil witch."

"Selfish hag."

"Soul-stealer."

"May you live out your days alone and unloved."

"Please, oh Queen, I'll do anything. Don't leave me here," she pleaded.

Cecella announced in a formal tone. "It's out of my hands. You were found guilty of all your crimes and are sequestered here for eternity. To add to your punishment, I want you to watch as I restore these women and they become mermaids to join us in spreading goodwill, to help the seafarers on their journey, a safe haven in the storm. They will have a life, one you rejected, and they will be happy."

One by one, Cecella called their names, waved a wand over them, watched the transformation into beautiful and colorful mermaids, their iridescent tails shimmering in the sunlight as they floated from the ship, and joined the pod under Cecella's reign.

When the final one assumed her position with the others, the Queen turned to her. "You will have a long time to ponder on your transgressions. Death will not come, even though you wish it. That is your curse."

Rose reached out again. "I'll change, I'll make amends, I'll do anything, but please don't leave me here." And then, in a croaking whisper begged, "At least restore my stone."

Even before she said the last word, Queen Cecella transformed and claimed her place in front of the pod.

In an instant they disappeared.

Desolation filled her. She wept as a child who lost their favorite toy. The vessel took on an eerie empty feel. A chilling cold seeped into her bones. *I am alone…utterly alone on this forsaken ship.*

As she looked out over the water, hoping to see the mermaids return, a transformation formed within and steeled the black thing called a heart. The tears dried up and defiance settled on her thin lips. She whispered fiercely to the open sea. "I'll beat this. This old barge can't hold me. I'll find a way. Yes, I will find a way."

She turned around and spoke to the empty room. "You forgot one thing, oh smug Queen. The opal in the mirror. It's still there and if I can extract its power, I'll leave here and seek my revenge on those who wronged me."

The day waned, making way for a clear night and a full moon.

The panic and despair she experienced earlier gave way to hope and thoughts of the vengeance she'd bestow upon each one who dared have a part in her imprisonment. That included Maren, Drake, and Captain Nelson. "They'll pay. And they'll never see it coming."

She went to the mirror to search the surface for the imbedded opal and gasped at the ghastly reflection. Always confident about her beauty, the face, drawn and white, was unrecognizable, the once rich auburn hair hung dull and lifeless, and the vivid blue eyes now muddied with gloom. Again, despair threatened to derail the fleeting determination she clung to moments before. *I'll deal with this later. The most important thing is to find the stone.*

Over and over, her hands ran across the surface of the mirror, certain she'd feel the place where the opal rested.

It isn't here. The glass is too smooth.

"How can the stone be gone?" she called out. Despair jeopardized any shred of resolve. She fought off the blackness with sheer force of will and did what she does best. Plot the next move.

Resourceful when needed, she stopped to ponder the options. *There's always a back door portal. This old bucket of rotten boards must have one. The trick is finding it.*

The rise and fall of the ship made her uneasy. *I hope storms aren't on the horizon. How I hate them. Underwater is much easier to tolerate than above.*

She smoothed the unkempt locks falling loosely in the wind, ran both hands over the rumpled dress and decided to find something to eat. *I'll be logical about this, and I always think better on a full stomach.*

The fully stocked galley functioned as a form of comfort. She spoke aloud, as the sound of her voice bolstered the fragile resolve deep within. "Good. I won't starve. Guess I should be thankful for that anyway."

Too hungry to cook, she made a ham sandwich, added tomato and a dab of rich butter. Tea was in the icebox, and she guzzled a whole glass before she took a breath. "Didn't realize the extent of my hunger and thirst." She dabbed her mouth with a napkin. "Now, I can gather my thoughts better."

Fresh made coffee simmered on the stove, so she poured a cup, carried it to the deck, and gazed out to sea. The clouds became darker, the breeze picked up, and a sprinkle of rain dampened her hair. The storm intensified making it difficult to stand. The ship tossed her around, the wind threatened to blow everything over. *Is this more of Cecella's punishment? I best go below and start looking for the back door portal.*

Before she could escape the downpour completely, rain pelted her relentlessly as she scurried down the stairs. Soaked, she looked for something to wrap around her body for a bit of warmth. After searching in several rooms, she found a linen closet. A half-dozen multi-colored quilts, neatly folded, offered the solution.

Warmer now, she continued the search. *There's a portal here somewhere, I'm sure of it.*

Nothing came of the time spent below, so she decided the gateway must be in another part of the ship. The storm raged on, causing the schooner to heave back and forth in a sickening manner. Exhausted, she longed for the comfortable rooms above deck, but couldn't chance it because of the deluge. She heaved a huge sigh. "I'll have to wait until this monsoon is over and find accommodations down here."

The quarters, dark and foreboding, offered little comfort especially since no lanterns seemed to exist in this part of the vessel. Left with no recourse she chose a room near the hatchway, propped the door open, and curled up in a corner to await calmer seas. *At least I have this warm quilt, that's something. How I miss my opal. If only I had the stone, I could conjure whatever I needed. I could even calm the tempest raging above. But, for now, I am powerless, but I won't remain so. There's a portal somewhere. I'll find it.*

As the storm raged on through the night, she slept. The open door of this room reassured her she'd awaken when the disturbance ceased.

Lulled to sleep by the rocking of the ship, and wrapped in the warm quilt, the coffee cup fell to the wooden floor with a thud. She didn't stir.

The rain did stop after a few hours, but she was oblivious, sleeping deeply from pure exhaustion.

As daylight approached, a sliver of sunlight passed over the crack of the closed hatch leading below. It wasn't much, and moved very quickly, leaving the rooms once again in the darkness. The gleam of light exposed Rose's one chance to be free, a tiny opal.

Eventually she woke, rested, hungry, and a bit warmer since

the storm dissipated. She folded the patchwork blanket carefully and returned it to the linen closet where she found it.

The cabinet door closed on the small opal safely tucked away in the hem of the very thing which warmed her through the night.

One small sparkle twinkled briefly while she'd slept. Sewn into the thin satin hem of the quilt, the small gem, barely perceptible to the naked eye, glowed in the miniscule fragment of light which passed over the hatchway, a fleeting shaft of brilliance she did not see.

CHAPTER TWENTY-SEVEN

MAREN HIT THE SANDY BEACH WITH A THUD, ARMS STILL entwined with Drake's and Captain Nelson's. Nausea threatened to overcome her, so she kept her eyes closed for a moment, the damp sand seeping through the back of her blouse. *Okay, it's obvious I'm not a time traveler. Nope, not my cup of tea.*

After a moment of fighting the ascent of bile in her throat, her lids fluttered open. Through the slits of her half-opened eyes, she saw Drake's arm on the right and Nelson's on the left interlocked with hers.

Neither man moved.

Fearful they didn't survive the chaotic odyssey which brought them home, she fully opened one eye and took stock of each man. Drake's mouth was slack, half-opened, but his chest moved up and down with each breath. *He's alive, at least.*

Still fighting the queasiness, she turned her head to assess Captain Nelson. His eyes were opened and staring at the sky. Alarmed at the sight, her gaze went to his chest fearing the worst. The rise and fall of his breathing, almost imperceptible, reassured her he was alive, as well. The breath she held released in relief. "Captain, are you awake? Can you hear me?"

The voice, hoarse and faint, replied, "Yes, I think I am indeed alive."

"Excellent," she answered. "Drake's still out. Can you move?"

He lifted his free hand. "A bit. Head's still foggy."

She extracted her arm from his, did the same with Drake, then attempted to sit up. "Just lie quietly for a minute. It will pass. The important thing is we all made it."

He issued a grunt and closed his eyes.

Her attention moved back to Morgan.

Drake's eyes blinked open, his voice weak and shallow. "Did we make it?"

"We're safe and alive. Be still, give yourself a few minutes to let your body adjust from the time travel," she instructed.

After a quick stock of their position, she reassured her companions. "We're on our home beach, right in front of your cabin, Drake. The stars are out and there's a full moon. Early evening is my guess."

Drake struggled to sit up. "Malcolm…where's my dog?" he asked no one in particular, his voice urgent.

"We'll find him. You must recover first," she said.

He moaned but remained upright, his gaze searching the beach.

Nelson managed to sit up and cover his face with both hands. "I'm too old for this kind of thing," he moaned.

The urge to chuckle at the two men almost overrode common sense. *This isn't the time to chide them, big strong men as they are. We're all lucky to have made it through in one piece.* She struggled to her feet and scoped the beach in both directions.

Drake managed to stand upright before Nelson and reached out to the old Captain. "Let me help you up."

Nelson gave him a half-grin and clasped Drake's hand.

All three, now on their feet, surveyed their surroundings.

"Over there," Maren said, "I see a light in my cabin. Maybe Telsa is there. Let's head that way."

"Wait," Drake interrupted. "I need to make sure Malcolm

isn't in my cabin. We're already here. Let's check it first, then we'll head to yours."

"Sure," she agreed. "Makes sense."

They followed him to the front door.

"Wait here, won't take me but a minute."

Nelson and Maren stood at the bottom of the steps while Drake searched inside.

He came out dejected. "He's not here."

"If Telsa is at my cabin, she might know what happened to Malcolm."

"Let's go." Drake led the way at a half run.

"Take it easy," she called after him. "We're not fully recovered from our ordeal. Remember, it takes a little bit to feel steady again."

The warning didn't deter Drake as he trudged toward the lighted cabin. He stumbled, fell to the ground, shook his head, and fought his way vertical again.

"Drake," she called. "Slow down. The captain can't move well. I may need your help. A few more minutes won't make a difference. Please," she begged.

He hesitated, but with slumped shoulders waited for them to catch up. "Sorry, I've never been away from Malcolm this long. I have to find out if he's okay."

"I understand, but we need to do this together. We're here for you, but Captain Nelson can't keep up with us," she said.

Nelson was out of breath and struggled in the damp sand.

Drake took his arm and the three continued forward to Maren's cabin.

They climbed the steps together.

Maren looked at Drake and Nelson, sighed deeply, and knocked on the door.

Footsteps echoed; a muffled woof came from deep inside the cabin.

The door opened and Telsa greeted them, eyes bulging, mouth open. "Maren!"

Before anyone else could say anything, a large dog sped past Telsa and landed smack on Drake propelling him down the stairs and flat on his back. Malcolm straddled his owner licking his face relentlessly.

They all laughed at the sight, but Maren turned back to Telsa. "That's one mystery solved. I'm so glad you found him and took him in. Drake would be lost without that dog."

"The dog is fine, what in the hell happened to you two? And who is this?" Telsa asked.

The joyful whining from Malcolm continued while Drake struggled to his feet.

"Oh, pardon me, you've not met Captain Nelson." She turned and made the introductions. "He's been captive on *The Lost Opal* for more than two hundred years," Maren explained.

"Lovely to meet you captain, but *The Lost Opal*? Two hundred years? I don't understand," Telsa replied.

"Of course, but it's too long of a story to tell standing out on the porch," said Maren.

Drake, with one hand on the scruff of Malcolm's neck, said, "I can't thank you enough for taking Malcolm in. How did you find him?"

Telsa smiled at the trio. "Like Maren said. Long story. Come inside. I'll make some coffee and sandwiches. I bet you all can use some sustenance."

Malcolm didn't leave Drake's side and nudged anyone who moved too close to his master.

"Gosh, I missed this guy. He doesn't look any worse for the wear, in fact, he looks as though he's gained weight. Spoil him much?" Drake grinned at Telsa.

"He was easy to spoil. I could tell he missed you though.

Sometimes he'd just sit at the front window looking out and whine. How do you explain your disappearance to a pet?"

"Tell us what happened after Rose sent me into oblivion," Drake asked.

Telsa went over the events directly after Drake disappeared, how she escaped Rose's grasp, how she found Malcolm, even how she levelled a rifle at the evil mermaid until the cops arrived.

"Bravo, Telsa! So, the police took her into custody? I bet that was interesting," Maren said.

Telsa continued, "No. They tried, but she disappeared right in front of all of us. That was a week ago. We've had no sign of her since. The police come back every day to ask me if I've seen her. I think they are suspicious of me."

Maren frowned. "She showed up yesterday on *The Lost Opal*. Where was she the rest of the time?"

"We may never know," said Drake.

They all fell into a silent reverie while coffee was poured, and sandwiches devoured.

"Okay, you guys. Your turn. What is *The Lost Opal*?" Telsa asked.

Maren told the story of Captain Henry Nelson and Rose's attempt to lure him into a love connection in order to remain on land. "Over two hundred years have passed. We finally have him off that horrid ship."

Nelson interjected, "We can't ascertain what's going to happen to me. This isn't where I came from. I should have gone back to the time I was abducted, but the only way to get off the ship was to travel with Maren and Drake. I warned them I might die in the process, but here I am. Not sure what will happen next. I could just disappear in a cloud of dust soon."

Telsa handed him a sandwich. "We pray that doesn't happen." She patted his arm.

Drake yawned. "I'm beat. Time travel really takes it out of

you. Think I'll head back to my cabin and get some sleep. I'll take Malcolm off your hands. Thanks again for taking such good care of him."

"My pleasure. He's a wonderful dog," answered Telsa.

"Well, I'm home, so I guess I'll turn in, too," Maren said.

Captain Nelson shifted his weight from one foot to the other, turning his gaze to each person in a befuddled manner.

Maren noticed his discomfiture and raised her eyebrows at Drake.

Drake was quick to catch her meaning. "Hey, Captain. I have two bedrooms. Why don't you bunk with me until we figure things out?"

Relief spread across the old captain's face. "Yes, yes, that's sounds like a plan. I'm extremely tired."

Telsa broke in, "Why don't you take my SUV, Drake. The captain doesn't look strong enough for another hike across the sand." She tossed the keys to Morgan.

"Great idea, thanks, Telsa. Come on, Captain. Let's leave before the women ask us to clean up the dishes."

"SUV?" Nelson asked.

"I'll explain when we're outside."

Morgan hurried Nelson out the door, Malcolm between them.

Before Drake followed Morgan, he turned, looked directly at Maren, and winked with a slow smile lighting his face.

She knew what that wink meant and gave him one back.

Telsa took the plates out of Maren's hand. "You're exhausted, my friend. You need to explain more about this time travel, but not tonight. Leave the dishes. You need rest. Plenty of time tomorrow to tell all about it."

Grateful, Maren didn't argue as she headed for the guest room.

Telsa reached out her hand. "No, I'm sleeping there.

Couldn't bring myself to disturb your room. Everything's just as you left it."

"You're the best, girlfriend."

Maren sat down on the bed, ready to pull off her shoes and lie down. Through the window she spied the taillights of Telsa's vehicle heading to Drake's cabin. She couldn't tell if exhaustion weakened her thoughts or if desire emboldened them. *Wish I was in that SUV with Drake, walking up the stairs, entering his bedroom, snuggling beside him while he holds me in his arms…*

The taillights winked off as she watched. It was too dark to see the men head into the house though, so she closed the blinds and succumbed to the tiredness of her body. *Will Drake still feel as he did on the ship come daylight or will real time change his perspective on our situation? His wink gave me some reassurance, but he might have second thoughts in the morning.*

CHAPTER TWENTY-EIGHT

C APTAIN HENRY NELSON JERKED AWAKE AS DAWN EMERGED from the fading night and revealed the very top of the spherical orb otherwise known as the sun. A quick pat of his person reassured him he was still intact. "Good, I didn't disappear into nothingness overnight." He sat up and stretched his arms above his head. "Well, I'll be hanged if I don't feel ten years younger than when I laid my head down last night. Amazing what a solid night's sleep will do to restore one's soul," he said to the empty room.

Dressed in only his knickers, he swung his feet out of bed and reached for his clothes, muttering, "Can't go around in these rags for too long. Everyone will think me daft."

As he pulled on his breeches, the stone bumped against his leg. "What? Oh, I almost forgot. The opal." He reached in his pocket and pulled it out, staring at it like a puzzle he couldn't solve. "Tarnation, what am I going to do with this?"

As if in answer to his question the oval gem glowed in the palm of his hand, then faded back into its natural state.

"Blimey, what does that mean? I'm too afraid of Rose's magic to decipher the meaning alone. I'll show it to Drake." He stuffed it back into his pocket and finished dressing.

Satisfied all was in place, he ran a hand through his graying hair before donning the final touch, the captain's cap. "Better take a quick gander in the mirror."

A quick assessment of the room disclosed the shaving mirror in the corner next to the window. He stroked the heavy beard adorning his face. "Time for that later, I'm dog hungry. Hope Drake is up." As he leaned into the mirror, he jerked back and peered over his shoulder as if someone stood behind him. "Who?" he sputtered.

He looked again.

The image reflected was a version of himself, but younger.

No graying mane. His beard, black as the night sky, gleamed as it once did years ago.

He turned around to see what manner of joke this was but found no one there taunting him. "This cannot be." He turned back to the reflection.

The younger image stared at him, eyes wide with wonder and disbelief. He patted his beard, his hair, and even his clothes, which appeared newer than they'd been for years.

Shocked, he called out, his gaze glued to the mirror, "Drake…Drake," he shouted louder.

The door flew open, and Drake burst in. "What's the matter, did you…" His mouth went slack, the sentence unfinished.

Neither man spoke, simply stared at each other.

Twenty seconds passed.

Drake broke the silence first. "Are you…are you Captain Nelson?"

The old captain could only nod.

Drake ventured further, "How did this happen?"

Still silent, Nelson pulled the opal from his pocket and held it out to Drake on the flat of his hand.

Drake stared at the jewel. "How…?"

"I stuffed the thing in my pocket and forgot about it." He lowered his hand and closed his fist around it. "I suppose the stone is responsible for my change in looks." He glanced back in the mirror, then returned his attention to Drake. "I don't know how, but there's no other explanation for this." He gestured at his hair and beard.

Drake recovered and smiled. "Well, the look is magnificent on you. This must be what you were like all those years ago."

"I don't know, Drake. I'm a bit aghast. What if each day I wake up and am a bit younger until I disappear altogether? Like dying slowly—until I cease to exist."

"Now, now. Don't borrow trouble. You don't know that is the case. We'll see tomorrow if you change any more. Meanwhile, you need to eat and…" He raked his gaze over Nelson's clothes. "…find you some other duds to wear. Come on. Coffee is on, and I bet Maren and Telsa will be here soon."

The kitchen was drenched in sunlight by the time Nelson sat down and took a gulp of the strong coffee Drake shoved in front of him. The black liquid almost scalded his throat as it slithered down, but he didn't mind. *I'm fortunate to feel anything at this point.*

Drake's staring eyes began to bother him. "Can you not goggle at me as if I have three heads. It's very disconcerting."

"Sorry, old chap. Can't help it. You remind me of my great-uncle. I only saw pictures of him, but you're a dead ringer.

Nelson's head jerked up.

Drake apologized, "Oh sorry. Poor choice of words. Anyway, I have this strange feeling we are kin somehow."

He studied Drake's face. "By Jove, there is some likeness. What was your great-uncle's name?"

Drake opened his mouth to answer, but Maren's voice interrupted.

"Anyone up? Time's a wastin.'"

"Come on in," Drake invited. "We're having coffee."

Maren preceded Telsa into the kitchen. "I'm glad to see

you're …" She stopped abruptly and Telsa bumped into her. "What? Who…Captain Nelson?"

"That's right, my dear. In the flesh. And a younger version to boot." The old captain acknowledged as he turned around for inspection.

"But how?" Telsa chimed in. She'd pushed in front of Maren to gawk.

"The stone," Drake answered for Nelson. "He had it in his pocket during our travel. We figure it's what triggered his transformation."

Maren sputtered; fear reflected in her voice. "The opal might be dangerous even in our hands. We really don't know how to use it. What of the captain's future? Will he disappear or will he just die?"

Nelson spoke first, "Sink me, Maren, don't gawk as if I'm ready to feed the fish. I'm feelin' fine at the moment."

"Sorry," she said. "Kind of a shocker, ya know?"

Drake pulled two stools out and indicated the women should sit. "I'll pour some coffee."

Both ladies sat down without taking their eyes off the phenomenon.

Telsa picked up the mug Drake offered, still staring at the new and improved captain. "So, you simply woke up this way?"

"Yes," he answered. "I woke energized with a vigor I've not known for years. Cast it off as a good night's sleep. I even dressed before I decided to take a look-see at my image in the shaving mirror. I was hornswoggled at the sight of me! I hollered for Drake, and well, here we are."

"Amazing," Telsa whispered.

"We have to find out how this stone works. I hate to be a downer, but we could say or do the wrong thing and create havoc, maybe even bring Rose back accidentally," Maren declared as she sipped her coffee. "Any ideas?"

No one spoke as they cast furtive glances between them.

Drake went to the refrigerator and pulled out eggs, cracked them into a bowl, and prepared the makings of a large omelet. Tomatoes, green peppers, onion, bacon. He chopped, whisked, and added salt and pepper.

Still, no one broke the silence.

He poured the concoction into an omelet pan and settled it on the preheated skillet.

Captain Nelson cleared his throat.

Everyone turned to look at him.

"We can contact Queen Cecella one more time."

CHAPTER TWENTY-NINE

Telsa Stewart studied Captain Henry Nelson carefully. The transformation from the day before made her head spin. Her assessment of the old sea captain filed him under 'sweet old man.' But this morning a different guy stood before her. His face once mottled and slightly puffy, now taut, tanned, and youthful. His gray hair transformed to ink black curls, the belly paunch gone, and the dull nut-brown eyes sparkled with new life, now a polished mahogany. The resemblance between Drake and Captain Nelson was not lost on her.

She blinked.

"I'm seeing this, but not believing it. Am I in a dream of some sort? And who is Cecella?" she asked.

Drake interjected before Nelson could answer, "Hey Captain, will you set out the silverware on those placemats for everyone. First drawer on the right."

"Certainly." Nelson moved across the room, opened the drawer, retrieved silverware, and placed forks and knives on each of four gray basket-woven placemats before he addressed Telsa's question. "The Queen of the Mermaids. She lives in the sea. We've summoned her twice before so I'm not sure she'll come again. I'm afraid my fate is in her hands." He paused without looking at anyone. "We have to try."

She thought a flicker of fear flashed over his face. "Are you frightened about this, Henry?"

His head snapped up and he locked his gaze with hers. "Frightened? No. However, if there is a chance I can stay here and get to know *you* better I want to take it."

Drake served up the omelet and refilled everyone's coffee before planting himself next to Maren. He glanced between Telsa and the captain. "We have many questions for Cecella, of course. One is what's to become of Nelson and another, what do we do with the stone? Before we summon her, let's make sure we have gone over all the possible inquiries we might have of her. Might not get another chance."

Telsa couldn't tear her gaze from Nelson. *God, he's so handsome.*

Maren sipped from her coffee mug. "I agree. Do we need paper, pencils?"

Drake shook his head. "No. I think we need to separate, divide and conquer so to speak." He stood, wiping his mouth with a napkin. "Maren and I will clear the kitchen. Telsa would you take the captain on a stroll down the beach? The two of you can come up with your own questions, then we'll meet up and compare notes."

Telsa slid off the stool and carried her plate to the sink, hiding the heat that rose to her face from the others. "I'm happy to. Are you sure I can't help with the dishes?"

"No, Maren and I have this. You…"

"Avast, ye buckos. Belay your plans. I'm not going to be gawked at by other land lubbers in these rags. If Rose lurked about, she'd be sure to spot me," Nelson reiterated.

"Right," Drake answered. "Come with me."

When the men left the room, Telsa's gaze followed them.

Maren giggled. "Falling for him much?"

Telsa swiveled away from the sink. "What? Who are you talking about?"

"I see the blush on your face. Drake is taken, as you well know, so of course I mean *Henry* as you call him now." Maren smiled. "He certainly is handsome."

Telsa stuttered, "Well, everything is so confusing. I'm overwhelmed, like in a dream. Last night he was a sweet old sea captain, now he's a dashing swashbuckler. I swear, my emotions are all over the place."

Maren nodded. "I felt the same when I first met Drake." She paused. "Let's do the dishes while we wait on them."

The kitchen was cleaned up and the girls perched on their barstools when the men returned. What they saw stunned them both.

They came in together, side by side.

Malcolm woofed and rose to all fours.

"Well, what do you think? No one will gawk at him now," Drake said.

But that is exactly what the two women did.

Telsa spoke first, "My God, you two could pass for brothers."

Captain Henry Nelson looked about thirty-five, decked out in white chino pants, a teal polo shirt, white slip-on deck shoes, no socks, and topped with a white and black beach-style nautical captain's hat with gold embroidered emblems.

He'd given the stone to Drake for safe keeping.

"The transformation is amazing," Maren said.

"Perfect," Drake agreed. "Now, enough ogling. We need to make a plan."

"Are you ready for that walk down the beach, Henry?" Telsa hopped off the stool and offered an arm to the newly transformed captain.

"I really like that you call me Henry. No one uses my given

name. I'm always Captain or Nelson." He took her arm as they strolled out the front door.

⇒✦⇐

"Should I be jealous?"

Drake's voice stirred her from the thoughts swirling in her mind as she watched her best friend saunter out the door with a two-hundred-year-old man.

"What? No, of course not. All of this is … so hard to believe. Is this really happening?" she said.

"Oh, it's happening. But we're not out of the woods yet. We're in possession of the opal and need to decide what to do with it. It could destroy us, or the captain, even Telsa," he replied. "Plus, someone is bound to see you or me, there will be questions as to where we were. We're taking a chance being seen right now until we figure this out. The authorities need to know we're back, but how will we explain all that happened? They'll throw us in the loony bin. We must come up with a plausible explanation to our disappearance and sudden return."

She turned to him and focused. "Yes, you're right. Anything come to mind?"

He moved toward her. "One thing."

She held her breath when she caught the whiff of his cologne. *Nautica Aqua Rush.* The same fragrance he always wore. The scent was fresh, energetic, and so him.

He was close now, took her chin in his hand and bent his head for the kiss. Long and deep, but tender and soul stirring.

When he released her, she took a moment to catch her breath and whispered, "I like that idea."

"More where that came from," he said in a low voice.

"Wait," she said. "I have to know. Was what happened on the ship real? Now that we're back do you feel the same?"

"You couldn't tell by that kiss?" he asked.

She ducked her head to hide the blush she sensed spread across her face. "Things can change when circumstances do. We thought that old tub was our fate. Maybe we didn't have any other choices."

He tipped her chin up. "Look into my eyes, Maren. I'm hopelessly in love with you. Have I not said it a thousand times?"

She locked her eyes with his. "Actually, no. You haven't said it even once."

His hand still holding her chin, he furrowed his brows, eyes burning into hers. "I haven't? I thought I surely had. Not once?"

"No," she said softly.

"Then I must correct that." He tightened his grip. "I love you, Maren Raybourn. I love you deeply, completely, and with a passion I've never known before."

She blinked. "I love you, too, Drake Morgan."

He kissed her then, deep, until her soul stirred.

They pulled apart, eyes locked, lips burning.

"Have dinner with me tonight. Just us. At that small bistro in town. *The Pink Seashell*," he said.

"What about Telsa and …"

"They can manage fine without us. Say you will."

She nodded.

"Great. I have to walk Malcolm. Want to come? No one will be on this part of the beach this morning, so no fear of being seen. Since you and Telsa buttoned up the kitchen, there's nothing keeping us inside." He laughed. "Perfect timing on my part."

"We had to do something while you two preened. You're worse than women," she answered.

While they strolled watching Malcolm check everything on the beach, they talked about the plans for the opal.

She had a hard time concentrating on the darn stone, however. *What is this dinner about?*

He was saying…"So, I think I should be the one to hang on to it. I can handle Rose if she finds a way back. Meanwhile, we'll talk to the others before we summon Cecella. See if we're all on the same page."

She forced her mind to concentrate on his words. "If you think that is best."

"Well, it's the only solution. If we leave it in Nelson's hands, she might find it more easily. And I don't want you or Telsa in any danger," he continued. He pointed toward the other end of the beach. "Here they come."

Sure enough, Nelson and Telsa came toward them, arm in arm, laughing, heads together.

"I surmise there's a bit of bonding going on there," Drake said.

"I'm worried. What if she falls for him and he disappears? Her heart will be broken. Not sure she can handle that," Maren mused.

"Which is why we should contact Cecella," Drake stated flatly.

"Ahoy mates," Nelson called. "It feels shipshape to walk on land again, even in this blasted sand."

Maren smiled at the glow on their faces. "Looks like the brisk sea breeze did you both some good."

"The air was certainly exhilarating," Telsa said.

"You sure it wasn't the company?"

"Okay, Maren, not the most subtle insinuation," Telsa shot back.

Drake intervened, "We need to put our heads together and figure this out. I believe we are still in danger. We've also been discussing how we're going to explain our sudden return and why we disappeared in the first place."

Nelson released his grip on Telsa's hand. "You're right,

Drake. Before any of us can move forward, we need to resolve this situation one way or another."

Maren opened her mouth to speak but refrained when she glimpsed surprise cross Drake's face.

He glanced at all of them, held up a hand and with the other reached inside his pocket.

The stone glowed with a vibrant orange light as it rested in his outstretched hand.

Maren shuddered.

Drake spoke softly, "We may have run out of time."

CHAPTER THIRTY

"SHALL WE START WITH COFFEE BEFORE WE BEGIN?" MAREN asked.

Drake shook his head. "I need a soft drink. Anyone else?"

She noticed the confused look on Henry's face.

"What is this soft drink you talk about?" he asked.

"Let me get you one," Drake offered. "This I gotta see."

He retrieved a can of Coke from the refrigerator and popped the lid. After filling a glass with ice from the icemaker, he poured the beverage and watched Henry's face scrunch and his mouth drop open as it fizzed over the crackling frozen cubes.

"You expect me to drink that? It resembles a potion of some sort," Henry exclaimed.

Everyone laughed.

Drake reassured him, "It's harmless, unless you count the amount of caffeine they put in this stuff. Go on, try it."

"Caffeine? Is that some kind of poison?" He gripped the glass and tipped it to his nose, giving it a bit of a sniff. "The bubbles remind me of champagne, although I rarely had the privilege of imbibing."

"Go ahead, taste it, Henry. It's incredibly delicious," Telsa urged. "You can trust me. I wouldn't let you drink it otherwise."

He smiled, took a sip, raised his eyebrows as he swallowed, then grinned. "Very interesting. A pleasant flavor."

Maren smiled at Henry's reaction, pleased he tried new things, but the urgency of their situation brought her back to the reason they sat around the bar. "Okay, back to the original subject."

"Right," Drake agreed. "Questions. Who wants to start?"

Maren went first. "Priority is Henry. We need to make sure nothing happens to him. Is the opal the key here?"

Everyone murmured their agreement except Henry who lifted the glass and peered into it as if to find its secret.

"Captain Henry, what's your opinion of the stone being in our possession?" she asked.

He tore his gaze from the fizzing beverage and studied Maren. "I feel we are relatively safe as long as *we* have the opal." He paused before he turned his head toward each of them one by one, his words deliberate and serious, "Unless…there is another stone."

She shuddered at the thought. "An excellent reason to contact Cecella and find out."

"Agreed, then there's Rose herself. Are we safe from her? Can she get off the ship without this stone?" Drake continued. "What other powers could she possess that will enable her to transport herself?"

"All relevant questions. Now we need to ascertain the right time to contact the Queen. Thoughts?" Maren asked.

"Let's do it tonight, close to midnight. That way no one else will be around," Drake suggested.

"I'm in," Maren agreed. "Everyone?"

"Sounds good," Telsa chimed in.

"Aye, this old sea dog agrees," Henry said. "Maren, she appeared when you summoned the last time. You should be the one to call her."

She nodded. "Makes sense to me."

Drake cleared his throat with a loud harrumph. "I'd like to ask a favor." He glanced at Henry, then Telsa. "Can you two make it on your own this evening? Maren and I have something to do. We'll meet you on the beach about eleven-thirty."

Both cheeks flamed hot. *What's he up to?*

"Sure," Telsa answered. "Josh is hosting a clambake. He invited me, so I can bring Henry as my guest. He won't ask about you two because he doesn't know you're back yet. Shall I hold on to that bit of information for now?"

"Yes, that's perfect," Drake said. "Let's wait until after we contact Cecella. You can just introduce him as Henry Nelson, a friend from the city."

"Okay, and where are you headed?" Telsa gave a sly smile. "Something we should know about?"

"You'll know soon enough," Drake said.

Maren walked back to the cabin with Telsa, who chattered away about the upcoming events of the evening.

She smiled at her friend, glad to have reunited with her, happy everyone was safe, but more than a little concerned about Drake's invitation for dinner. *I wonder what he has planned.*

She didn't hear Telsa's question, didn't know she even asked one until she realized no one walked beside her. "What are you doing?" she asked her friend, who stood behind her, feet planted in the sand, hands on her hips.

"Waiting for an answer. You're a million miles away right now. What's going on, Maren?"

"I'm sorry." She trudged back to her friend, grabbed her hand, and pulled her along. "It's Drake. Says he wants me all to himself this evening. Dinner at *The Pink Seashell*. I'm wondering what it's all about, that's all."

Telsa let out a whoop. "Ooowee! If you can't figure it out, you're denser than I realized."

"Don't jump the gun."

"He's going to ask you to marry him. You *have* to know that. It's the only logical conclusion."

"The thought crossed my mind, but what if I'm wrong?"

Telsa laughed. "You're not. Now let's get back to the cabin and decide what you're going to wear tonight. Where are you going to have the wedding? Here on the beach? Surely not back in the city. Drake will never go for that. I'm going to be Maid of Honor, right?"

Maren let Telsa rattle on, while doubts crowded in her mind. *What else can it be but a marriage proposal? Or maybe he wants to rescind his declaration of love, let me down easy. Reveal he's decided to move on, take another ship and sail off into the wild blue yonder.*

At the cabin, while Telsa went through her closet, Maren studied her reflection in the mirror. *Pretty unremarkable, I'd say. Average face, okay complexion, I guess my green eyes are an asset, but what does Drake see in me?*

"Cut that out, Maren."

She jumped at the sound of Telsa's voice behind her. "What?"

"I know what you're doing. Analyzing your looks. Wondering what he's attracted to." Telsa placed a hand on her hip. "Am I right?"

A sigh answered the question. "I suppose you are. My silly lack of confidence is rearing its ugly head." She turned to her friend. "He's so handsome and I'm nothing special. What can he possibly see in me?"

"Oh, please. I'm not playing this game with you. For once in your life accept this is happening to you. Enjoy the ride. Trust in yourself," Telsa said. "Here, this soft green sundress will bring out your eyes. It's flirty, but not too revealing. Perfect for a marriage proposal."

They spent the rest of the morning choosing magical iridescent hoop earrings that sparkled with tiny opals, a pendant to match, and rock stud flat thong sandals tying it all together. They even argued about how she would wear her hair. She put her foot down at Telsa's suggestion she pull it into a ponytail. Fun girl time, like back in Seattle, before she became aware of mermaids, opals, and time travel.

They shared a sandwich of tuna and tomato at lunch and a wonderful cup of tea, the brew Telsa brought with her everywhere. She claimed it restored her sanity and calmed her nerves.

"Wonder what the boys are doing?" Telsa asked.

"Probably much the same as we are. I'm sure they've kept themselves amused with stories of their seafaring adventures," she answered.

They fell silent for a time.

"What's going through your mind now, Maren?"

"Marriage. I don't think I'm ready," she said.

"Look, an engagement is just that. An engagement. It can be long, or short. Your call. Take as much time as you need to be sure. It's not like you'll get married tomorrow."

"You're right, but should I even accept the proposal if I'm not open to it yet. I hardly know, him."

"Let's go out on the porch." Telsa pulled Maren from the kitchen bar stool.

They settled in the white wicker chairs facing the ocean.

"Look." Telsa pointed down the beach. "Drake's walking Malcolm."

Her eyes misted as she took in the sight. He threw a stick, and the exuberant dog ran after it bringing it back for his master to throw again. *Those two have such a bond.*

"Wonder where Henry is?" Telsa asked.

"Probably resting for his big date with you, tonight."

Telsa's nose wrinkled as she frowned. "It's not a date. Only a get-together."

"Oh, I get it. You can tease me, but I'm not afforded the same privilege?" she goaded.

"Well, the scenarios are different. Henry is over two hundred years old. We just met. Nothing's been declared like with you and Drake."

"Yes, but you find him attractive," Maren continued.

Telsa hesitated, "Well, yes, but what if he disappears, goes back to *his* time? I'm keeping close guard on my heart until we know more."

"Good idea."

The sound of Malcolm's barking distracted them. The dog planted all four feet toward the ocean yipping and snarling at the water.

Drake stood behind him trying to call him away.

Malcolm would have none of it.

That's when Maren noticed an orange glow emanating from Drake's pocket. Even from yards away, the glimmer was like a beacon on the beach.

"Do you see that, Telsa?"

"Yes, it must be the opal… and something's in the water. Malcolm can see it. You don't think Rose has returned, do you?"

"I hope not. Let's go find out."

They hopped off the porch and headed for the growling dog and Drake's illuminated pocket.

Maren waved toward him. "Drake, hey Drake. What's going on?"

Before they reached him a mirage formed on the water, not far from the beach.

"Stay back. Don't come any closer," Drake shouted.

CHAPTER THIRTY-ONE

D RAKE YANKED ON MALCOLM'S COLLAR AND COMMANDED him to heel. When the dog hesitated, he lowered his voice and ordered, "Now."

Malcolm immediately sat but continued a whining growl as his eyes riveted on the apparition in the water.

One hand on the collar and the other waving Telsa and Maren off, he tried to make out what churned on the water just yards away from him. "Malcolm old boy, I can't quite make it out. Is it a mermaid? Surely, not Cecella. Why would she show up without being summoned? Rose, maybe? But she has no stone, or does she?"

Malcolm yipped in response.

The illusion continued to come into some sort of focus until he could make out a woman from the waist up floating in the water, long hair in kaleidoscope colors drifting around her, eyes a piercing aquamarine.

She called out in a voice resembling the thrums of a harp, "You summoned?"

"I did?" he asked.

She pointed to the glow in his pocket.

He looked down, startled. Carefully, he drew the object from its hiding place.

"The opal is activated. I came to answer the call. My name is Lakelyn. How may I serve you?"

From his peripheral vision he saw Telsa and Maren inching forward, necks craning as if to make out the words. He didn't stop them this time, instead assessing this was a good time to request a meeting with Queen Cecella. "The Queen, are you of her court?"

"I am," she answered.

"We, uh, my friends and I request an audience with her. As you see I'm not a mermaid, yet I have this stone. It activated, as you say, without my knowledge. I'm unaware as to how this happened. How is it possible?"

"One with a strong will can instill life into an amulet such as you possess. Once the stone is in your possession, you own its power. I will convey your request to the Queen. Have you a time and place in mind?"

The women, now within feet of him, approached cautiously.

"Yes," he said. "Midnight at Passion Rock. Is that acceptable?"

"I will tender your request. If you do not hear from me again, the appointment is set." She cocked her head in a slight bow and said, "At your service."

Lakelyn disappeared in a swirling golden mist.

Drake continued to stare at the ocean while Malcolm barked once when the mermaid dissolved.

Maren broke the silence. "Wow, can you believe what just happened? Lakelyn is a beautiful name." She stared at Drake. "You have the power of the opal now. Does that mean Rose is gone forever, stripped of all her power? And what are you going to do with the stone?"

Drake shook his head, still staring across the water. "These are things we must ask Cecella. Not sure I want this power. What possible need do I have to own this thing? I must give it back."

"Don't discount anything until you understand what possessing the opal can do. The Queen will guide us," Maren said.

"But we're not mermaids." He ripped his gaze from the water and turned to her.

Telsa finally found her voice. "Maybe you don't need to be."

Henry's voice interrupted them. "I'm a little jittery about this appearance."

"You saw what happened?" Drake asked.

"Yes, I heard Malcolm barking. I watched from the porch, afraid they might have come for me," Henry said.

"That isn't why she appeared. Apparently I activated the opal simply by my will."

Malcolm nudged Drake's hand.

"Nothing more we can do until midnight. Lakelyn said she'd inform us if Queen Cecella is otherwise engaged. Not sure how she'll do that, but not my worry. The boy here is hungry. I need to feed him." He looked at his watch. "The afternoon is gone. Time to get ready for dinner." He glanced at Maren and winked. "I'll pick you up in an hour."

Telsa grabbed Henry's arm. "The clambake starts in half an hour. We can head that way now if you're ready. Quite a little hike to the other side of Maren's cabin."

"I'm honored to spend this time with you, Telsa. Might as well enjoy myself. Midnight might mean the end of my time here. I've got nothing to go back to if they do send me away." He addressed Drake and Maren. "You two have a pleasant evening. We'll see you at midnight."

Arm in arm, the old captain and Telsa trudged across the deep sand.

Drake spoke softly to Maren, "Will you be ready in an hour? I can hardly wait to have you to myself."

"Yes, I'll be ready," she answered.

He pecked her on the cheek, snapped his fingers at Malcolm,

and turned toward his cabin. Before he arrived at his porch, he glanced at the retreating figure of Maren almost to her bungalow. *I've always been a confirmed bachelor, but Maren has rearranged my thought process.*

"Come on Malcolm. Let's go dress. Life as we know it is about to change."

❧

Maren couldn't remove Lakelyn from her mind. *Is she for real or some trick proliferated by Rose? I guess we'll find out at midnight.*

While she shimmied into the green sundress her thoughts drifted to Drake. Her heart pounded with anticipation. *He's so handsome, so kind, so caring. Everything a woman wants in a man. I want him to ask the question, but I'm scared to death. And what of his newfound power? The silly opal. Will that piece of rock change him?*

She slipped on the last sandal and heard a knock. *Right on time.*

She let out a short gasp when she opened the door.

Drake filled the door frame, capless, raven black curls framing a tanned face, sorrel brown eyes dancing with excitement. Instead of his normal sailor garb, he sported a camel-colored blazer, a pale blue cashmere T, and navy chinos.

"C-come in," she managed to croak out the words, unable to catch her breath as she took in the view. He'd always dressed in sea-worthy garb. This cosmopolitan style blindsided her. She liked it. *Really* liked it.

Even though she managed to invite him in, he continued to stand in the doorway staring at her.

She grabbed his hand and drew him inside.

"Maren," he said, voice almost inaudible, raspy, and full of emotion. "You look…amazing."

"Thank you, you're pretty easy on the eyes yourself." Her

184

voice returned to normal, and she continued, "Do you want something to drink before we head out?"

"No, I can't wait for this date. Let's go now."

She nodded, grabbed her bag, and led the way out the door.

Neither spoke on the drive to the restaurant.

He glanced at her every couple of minutes, his dark eyes glittering in the dim light.

She stole glances and secretly smiled. *He looks so happy, and I feel the electricity between us. Do I dare believe he's really in love with me?* But her mind returned to the opal in his possession. *How can I give him an answer if he proposes marriage when I still don't know what this opal might mean in our lives? I won't find out until midnight. I wonder if it's in his pocket right now.*

He opened the car door and helped her out.

The Pink Seashell's warm atmosphere greeted them, and the fragrance of seafood and fresh bread made her stomach growl. The tuna sandwich from lunch was long gone.

The hostess guided them to a secluded table surrounded by seaweed and mermaid murals on the wall, all accented with twinkling lights. The candle on the table nestled inside a conch shell, the silverware handles adorned with small turtles on the end, and the spoons resembled seashells. All very conducive to the beach scene. No one acted as if they recognized them, an added bonus.

Drake pulled out her chair and she settled at the table.

"This is lovely, Drake. I love the décor."

He took his place across from her and reached for her hand. "You outshine everything in this room, Maren. You take my breath away."

She felt heat rise to her cheeks. "Thank you."

They sat for a moment, not speaking, just gazing at each other.

The hostess returned for their drink orders.

"How about a couple of mimosas to start?" Drake asked.

Maren nodded. When once more they were alone, she went against her instinct and blurted out, "Where is the stone, Drake?"

He started and blinked. "What?"

"The stone. Do you have it on you?"

"Well, yes, I decided not to leave it unattended. Better to be aware of what's happening with it, than not."

The emotions tumbled around in her brain. Disappointed the stone was so close but glad to know it was safe with him, the thing seemed to hover between them.

The twinkle left his eyes. "I didn't bring you here to discuss the stone, Maren. Time enough for that later tonight."

"I-I'm sorry. I'm worried is all. I suppose our safety is on my mind. Could Rose be here somewhere, waiting to send us to some unknown region? I just can't stop thinking about her."

The hostess brought their drinks.

Drake waited until she'd gone. "And I can't stop thinking about *you*."

She studied his face. A scar over his left eye jumped out at her. She'd never noticed it before. "How did you get the scar?"

He paused, blinked, then as though involuntary, lifted his hand to touch the long-healed mark. "Oh, that. A scuffle on the ship while out at sea. A deckhand didn't like an order I gave him. Drew a knife."

"Who won?"

He smiled. "I did. The bloke was let off at the next port. Why do you keep changing the subject?"

"Nervous, I guess."

The hostess appeared again, but Drake waved her off. She disappeared.

"Then I won't waste any more time. I was going to wait until after dinner, but your attention span is too short."

His smile melted her heart.

He slid from his chair, crouched on one knee, withdrew a small jewelry box, and opened it. "Maren Raybourn, will you marry me?"

She knew this was coming, sensed it from the first glimpse of him at the door. He vibrated with anticipation. But now that he was on one knee with a ring in his hand, she swallowed hard.

The ring was exquisite. The band, a gold rope. The setting, the same gold rope tied in some sort of sailor's knot with a huge princess-cut diamond resting in the middle. Her breath all but left her.

"Drake, it's beautiful," she whispered.

"I chose it especially for you."

"I'm not sure what to say," she said.

"Say yes," he countered.

"I-I- well…"

CHAPTER THIRTY-TWO

T HE CLAMBAKE PROVED A RESOUNDING SUCCESS, AND Telsa was glad she'd brought Henry. Everyone liked him from the beginning and enjoyed his seafaring stories, vague though they were—he gave away nothing.

She secured her arm through his, whispered it was time to go and suggested they bid farewell to their host.

Josh wrung the captain's hand, gave Telsa a brotherly hug, and invited them both to come again.

Her digital watch glowed the numbers eleven ten. *Time enough to slog through the sand to Passion Rock.*

"What an enjoyable evening," Henry said. "Good food, good friends. A perfect night."

"I enjoyed the company particularly." She squeezed his arm and smiled.

He pressed his fingers against her hand gently. "If this is to be my last night, I'm glad it was with you."

"Let's not think of that. Enjoy the walk and we'll deal with it when it comes," she said.

"But I must ask you…what if I am sent back to my time? You told me you have no family here, no husband, no children, no one. Only your job. I hate to think of you all alone here."

"Funny, I never thought much about that before. *Now I*

would feel exceptionally alone without you. Maybe you won't have to go back. You might have a choice in the matter."

He stopped and turned to her. "Telsa, I'm developing a deep regard for you. One might call it love. Whether I go or stay, I want you with me."

They stood in the sand, gazing at each other, searching, yearning.

Finally, she whispered, "I'd go anywhere with you."

"Back in time?" he asked.

"Anywhere," she answered.

"And your responsibilities as a publisher?"

"Anyone can do my job. I have any number of replacement prospects. Even Maren."

"Then we must consider you traveling back with me to my time as a request when we address Queen Cecella." He took her hand.

They walked in silence for a bit.

"Do you think Maren accepted Drake's proposal of marriage?" he asked.

"I hope so. She brought up all sorts of reasons why she wouldn't or couldn't. She thinks too much. Needs to let her heart lead sometimes."

"They genuinely love each other. You should have seen them on the ship. Couldn't keep their hands off one another." He chuckled.

"Well, the looks they exchange say it all."

Passion Rock came into view.

"The time has come," Henry said.

"Yes, and I see Maren and Drake." She pointed. "They're holding hands. That's a good sign."

Telsa waved at the pair approaching and tugged on Henry's arm. "Let's hurry. I can't wait to find out if she said yes."

The two couples arrived at the rock simultaneously, all four grinning.

Drake let out a huge whoop.

Maren held out her hand and displayed the magnificent ring.

"Congratulations to you both," Henry said as he shook Drake's hand.

Telsa wrapped her arms around her friend and let the tears fall. "I'm so happy for you. I was so afraid you'd talk yourself out of it." She pulled back and grabbed Maren's hand. "Let me see the ring again. How beautiful," she whispered. "You must tell me everything."

"I will," Maren said. "But not just now. We have an appointment, remember?"

Telsa turned somber. "How could I forget?"

Little was said as they positioned themselves in front of the rock.

Telsa's arm wound through Henry's.

Drake held Maren close.

They waited.

Nox viewed the scene at Passion Rock with trepidation, remembering the occurrence that led him here.

He'd been summoned.

Back at his cabin, a stone much like the one Rose had possessed lay hidden under the floorboards, gladly forgotten as the years passed. On this day, as he passed between the wood stove and the table readying things for supper, an amber light filtered through the cracks and caught his attention.

A weakness attacked his knees, and he almost lost his balance as fear sent a jolt to his heart. "A summons," he said in a muffled voice. "The last time that happened, it didn't end well."

The floorboard came loose with the use of a crowbar, but Nox hesitated before retrieving the stone. After a deep breath and an uneasy resolve, he pulled the thing from the open velvet-lined box, shaking all the while, set it on the table, and waited.

The glow intensified.

He backed away but jumped when a diaphanous form filled the door frame and spoke softly, "Queen Cecella requires your services. Midnight at Passion Rock."

"But I…," he began too late.

The shape dissolved.

"Bugger," he spat. "'Twasn't a request. She'll turn me into a toad or worse if I don't appear. I'd bet my own grandmam this has somethin' to do with that hag, Rose. I knowed she'd bring me trouble. If she'd found this stone, I'd never be rid of her. The old Juniper tree worked well enough to get her gone. At least she never came back, and I can only suppose the spell got her where she wanted to go." He stamped his foot. "Dang it. Thought I was done with all that."

He hadn't thought of Passion Rock in decades. The edifice was a portal known to all sorts of wizards and magical creatures. The thing was distasteful to him, as he wanted little contact with those worlds. He preferred his own company.

Now, here he stood watching events unfold at Passion Rock from a grove of trees on the hill.

Two couples approached the granite-like boulder with squeals of delight, hugs, and excited chatter.

"Botheration, what are those four ninnies doing here?" He crouched with his back against a tree and waited. "Ye old Queen won't approach with mortals hangin' about. I might be here for hours."

To his surprise, at the stroke of midnight, Cecella *did* appear. He stood, ready to find out what she wanted, but stopped when he saw her address the two couples.

The words were unintelligible from this distance, but he could tell she knew them.

They conversed for a few minutes, then a buzz filled his ears, and he heard the Queen's voice. "Approach," she said.

His old, crooked knees wobbled as he descended the hill.

Maren, Drake, Telsa, and Henry turned and watched his advance.

He gave a sidelong glance to the four mortals and kept a close eye on Queen Cecella. When he stood on the edge of the beach, waves lapping his feet, he gave a deep bow. "I received your summons my queen. I pray I haven't offended thee."

"No need for concern, Nox, my friend," Cecella replied. "I've brought you here because you are the 'Keeper of the Opal.' These four are my friends and victims of a grievous act against them from one called Rose."

Nox nodded at the group although no smile crossed his lips.

The queen continued, "You've had an encounter with her and managed it with exceeding dispatch. She is banished but her opal found its way into their hands. Because of its vast power, I am commending the stone into your keeping. Will you take possession of this amulet and keep it safe?"

He bowed deeply, again. "I accept this instruction with happiness to serve thee, my Queen."

"Captain Morgan, please hand over the stone."

Drake reached into his pocket, withdrew the opal, and handed it to Nox.

"Thank you," said the wizard. "I've heard your name before. May I ask the names of the others?"

"Certainly," he pointed to each of his friends as he called their name.

"Yes, I am aware of your plight. Happy to know no harm came to you."

Drake asked, "Thank you. We are relieved the stone is in your hands and not ours."

The opal glowed as he carefully slipped it into his pocket. "I will keep it safe. Do not fear." He turned back to Cecella. "Is my mission complete? May I return to my home?"

"Not yet. There is to be a marriage between Captain Morgan and Maren. They want to be united in matrimony before anyone else is aware of their return. The wedding ceremony is day after tomorrow, at midnight, right here by Passion Rock. They need a judge magistrate. You fulfill that capacity. I know you've officiated at other weddings. Will you agree?"

His eyes rounded; his jaw dropped. "Why, I've only performed in that capacity with those of our kind, never mortals."

Cecella pressed the matter. "But you do hold a certificate. I remember when you pursued it. You asked for my approval."

His knobby knees shook with trepidation. The last thing he wanted was to mingle with mortals. "Well, yes. In my younger years I was more involved in the community, those whose persuasion was consistent with ours. But now, most have moved off. I've not had cause to officiate in many years. I am very much alone on the mountain."

"Nevertheless, you are the only viable answer to this dilemma. We don't want to draw unnecessary attention to the mortal populace just yet," Cecella continued. "I'm asking a great deal of you, I know. This will be considered a great favor. One, I promise, I will never ask again."

He trembled, then sighed. "Then I cannot refuse such a gracious request."

Cecella bestowed a rare smile. "Thank you, my friend. You are free to go."

He bowed again, nodded at Drake and the others, and moved toward the hillside.

"Wait," Drake called to him. "We want to thank you."

Maren piped up, "We consider you a friend, as well as the queen and her mermaids. You are protecting us by keeping the opal. We will regard your part in our wedding an honor."

A curt nod sealed the deal. "I really must go." He turned abruptly and disappeared into the forest.

Henry took the lead before Cecella could disappear. "Oh Queen, we have one more appeal."

"Yes, Captain Nelson?" she asked.

"What of my situation? Am I to remain here, in this time?"

"You are here only temporarily. Seven days is the allotted period for time travelers in your position. Time to regain your strength before being transported back to your proper place. Is that a problem?"

"Well, yes. Telsa wants to come with me."

CHAPTER THIRTY-THREE

STRANGLED WORDS RIPPED FROM MAREN'S THROAT. "What? You can't…"

Henry interrupted her protest. "That is for Her Grace to decide my friend, and of course, Telsa."

Queen Cecella raised one hand to silence them. "This is a profoundly serious request, Captain Nelson. The historical fabric of your existence will be altered."

His brows furrowed; his lips formed a deep frown. "I understand the gravity of the situation, but we are willing to take the risk. If I can't stay here, then we want to be together in *my* time. Is it possible?"

The Queen settled her gaze on Telsa. "You want this?"

She nodded. "Very much."

"You have no family, nothing to tie you here, making your goal difficult to achieve?"

"Correct, no living parents, no siblings. I am basically alone here," she explained.

"Then I see no problem with your request. Your wish is granted." She continued, "You may take nothing with you. Only the clothes on your back, understood?"

"Yes, we understand. When will this transpire?" Nelson asked.

"After the wedding. Be ready," the Queen said.

Telsa and Henry grabbed hands and nodded.

Cecella disappeared in a swirl of water and moonlight before Maren could protest further whereupon she turned to her friends. "Wait, you can't do this. I won't let you. I need you here."

Exasperation and fear clouded Telsa's face as she blurted, "Do you hear yourself, right now?" said Telsa. "I, I , I. What about Henry and me? Have you given any thought to what we want?" Immediately, she reached for Maren. "I'm so sorry. I only meant…"

Drake raised one hand to interrupt Telsa, then put his arm around Maren and drew her close before he broke his silence, "She's right, darling. The decision is not up to us."

"But…," she tried to argue.

Telsa took her hand and said, "You have Drake. Your life will be glorious. I want this chance with Henry. Please be happy for us."

Tears blotched her cheeks as she thought about a world without her friend in it. They'd worked together for many years with Telsa acting as rudder throughout the creative process in her illustrations. Focus and clarity always came to the forefront when she reviewed her work. She kept her balanced. *How will I function?* But ultimately, this wasn't about her own need. They had a right to pursue happiness together.

She sighed, bit back the tears, and relinquished the fear their initial announcement fostered. "You're right. I'm being selfish." The crack in her voice made her whisper, "I just can't imagine life without you."

"Remember the things I taught you. The business will be yours now. I'll draw up the papers. We're such a small company, no one will notice I'm gone when you take over. You can even stay on the beach and run it from here. Everything is done remotely now anyway. Have faith in yourself, trust your instincts."

My instincts, she says. That's always the struggle. I've leaned on her to keep me on track. She let her gaze drift up to her new fiancé standing close beside her. *Surely my intuition is right about him.* A stiff breeze lifted a lock of hair and deposited the errant strand over one eye. In a brisk move, she shoved it out of her way. *Of course I'm right about Drake. We're meant for each other. If I'm so sure about him, why can't I feel as confident about my work? Telsa is forcing me to face these insecurities…and maybe it's time I did.*

She turned to Henry. "Forgive me for casting a shadow over your plans, Captain Nelson. I've come to value our short friendship as one of the most important in my life. You kept me alive, gave me hope when there was none. How I will miss you, but I will take comfort knowing you and my best friend are together. Your happiness will be a blessing I will cherish all of my life."

Henry wrapped his burly arms around her. "You are a survivor, Maren. I knew that the moment I laid eyes on you. I treasure our meeting for many reasons. Your loyalty, determination, and fighting spirit, and because you led me to Telsa. I will always carry you in my memory. Go and be happy, my dear. You have a perfect man in Captain Morgan."

In the end, Drake joined Maren and Henry with his arms encircling the two. Telsa completed the circle.

Tears flowed.

Finally, he stepped back and said, "Our love and thoughts will be with you forever, but may I remind you we have a wedding to plan."

The foursome broke apart wiping the teardrops streaming down their cheeks.

"He's right. If this is supposed to happen day after tomorrow, we need to begin," Telsa stated. "Where shall we meet to get this underway?"

Maren chimed in, "My place eight a.m.." She grabbed Drake's hand. "You have breakfast duty."

"On it!" he agreed.

At the precise stroke of eight a.m., Drake arrived with a bag of groceries nestled in his arm. Before he even deposited the parcel on the table, he swooped Maren up in a firm one-armed embrace and kissed her. "I'm making omelets, again."

Her joyful laughter brightened the kitchen and warmed his heart.

In short order, eggshells lay broken on the counter, the sound of whisking filled the room, onions and tomatoes were chopped, and Drake asked, "Can you hand me the cheese?"

Telsa poked her head through the open door. "Anybody up? I smell coffee."

Henry emerged through the front door and drew her inside the sunny kitchen. "Sit here while I pour you a cup." As he reached for the pot, he remarked, "Omelets again, huh? Good thing they're the best I've ever tasted. I'll really miss our time together and your omelets."

The foursome grew quiet at the reminder.

Finally, Drake broke the silence, "Order up! Dig in."

The cheddar-topped omelets lay side by side on a large platter.

Maren made a round with the coffee pot and sat down next to Drake. "I can't believe I'm going to marry such a talented cook. I'll be so spoiled."

He laughed. "Not so fast, my darling. Breakfast may be my forte, but there are two other meals in the day. I leave those to you."

"But…" she began.

"See here, you two, plenty of time to argue about that when you're hitched. We have to get you married first," Henry declared.

"So, the only ones attending will be the four of us, the mermaids, and Nox?" Drake continued.

Maren nodded. "I think all we need to be concerned about is what we'll wear and oh, flowers. The ceremony will be simple, but I would like a few traditional touches."

"How will we acquire a dress without alerting people you are back?" Telsa asked.

"We can browse online at a boutique. Have it delivered," Maren suggested.

"Great idea. Same for the groom," Telsa agreed.

Drake jumped in. "Oh no you don't. I'm wearing my uniform. Period."

Maren clapped her hands. "Oh yes, I hadn't thought of that. Superb notion."

Henry looked at his new love. "What about us? Any ideas on what we should wear?"

"Hmm," she mused. "Cecella said we'll probably do our little time travel bit right after the wedding and should only take the clothes on our backs. Which means we should dress according to the time to which we are returning. Thoughts?"

"You're right," Henry said. "But all I have is the old moth-eaten uniform I came here in."

Maren chimed in, "Again, we can search online for period costumes, something simple so as to not attract attention."

Drake collected the empty plates and placed them in the sink. "Sounds like you ladies have some work to do. Henry and I will clean this up."

Maren exchanged a glance with Telsa. "Ready to start?"

"Yep, let's go."

Drake called after them, "I'll take care of the flowers. Give you more time to shop."

"Lovely, thank you!" she answered.

"I like this one," Maren said in a low voice. "Kind of a bohemian look. What do you think?"

Telsa studied the picture for a second. "Looks like you, for sure. Let's call to see if they have it in stock and when they can deliver."

The girls had poured over the local boutique websites for over an hour before they settled on the free-spirited dress, a Chapel train tulle and lace design with an off-the-shoulder neckline and sheer sleeves. The overlayed skirt boasted sizable, embroidered flowers, and hit just at the ankle.

"Shoes?" Maren asked.

"Sandals. In the sand it will be hard to walk."

She called the boutique, and they assured her they had one in her size and available for delivery in the afternoon, along with a simple pair of white sandals.

"Now for you and Henry," she continued.

They found a website for vintage clothing and settled on something suitable.

For Telsa, a full, homespun skirt with petticoats in a soft brown, along with sturdy shoes.

"Not the most glamourous, but will serve you well when you travel back," Maren said. "We'll put flowers in your hair to add a more festive flare."

"I'm fine with it. All I want is to be with Henry," Telsa sighed.

They chose a ruffled linen shirt and breeches sans the long coat. They wanted to be simple so as not to attract attention wherever they landed. Instead of a tricorn hat, they opted for a leather cap. Add the long stockings and shoes, and they were all set.

"I have no idea if Henry will still be a captain or what his status will be when we arrive. We'll have to play it by ear."

"Are you nervous?" Maren asked.

"A little. But as long as we're together, I'll be fine. I think of it as a colossal adventure."

She paused, not sure she should broach the subject, but decided she had to. "And Rose? Do you worry about her return? Or if she already exists in that time, before all this happened? Before she banished Henry to the ship."

Telsa studied Maren's face before she turned to gaze out the window. "I can't think about that. Together we are strong. We'll figure things out as we go."

Maren grabbed Telsa's hand. "Yes, you're tough, but I will stay concerned. I wish there were some way for me to know if you are all right."

"Your job is to take care of Drake. And if possible, I'll try to find a way to send a message of sorts. Not sure how all that works. But please don't worry. Henry and I will be fine."

They were interrupted by Drake standing in the doorway in his uniform.

"Thought I'd better make sure it still fits. What do you think?"

CHAPTER THIRTY-FOUR

NIGHTS WERE THE WORST.

Rose felt especially alone after sunset. The days found her searching for an amulet or book of spells, anything she could use to get off the cursed vessel. So far, to no avail.

Half-heartedly, she shuffled downstairs to the galley and poured some coffee, sat down, cupped her chin in one hand, and shut her eyes. *I've been here more than a week and running out of options. I refuse to think there is no way off this ship. Just because Henry couldn't find his way off doesn't mean I can't.*

Her irritable mood caused her to kick over the chair as she jumped to her feet. She thrust it aside, grabbed her cup, and made her way up the stairs to the main deck.

A breeze cleared the fog in her brain and carried her spoken words to parts unknown. "Looks like rain, maybe a storm is brewing. I best prepare for the deluge."

Back in the galley, she gathered rolls, a jar of beef jerky, and plenty of tea. After placing everything in a basket, she hauled the staples upstairs and into the room she'd occupied during the last weather event. She hated storms. Never got used to them when she lived under the sea and was one of the reasons she wanted to leave that existence behind. To add to her unease within the pod, she never fit in with the other girls. *Goody goodies. Every one of them.* "Please the queen," she sneered. "Do her bidding. Simpering idiots."

She settled into her corner to await the storm but realized she'd forgotten a blanket. *Drat. Can't do without some kind of warmth.*

She hauled herself up with a groan and went to the cabinet in the hall. On top of the pile was the one she'd used before, folded neatly. She reached to grab the quilt when something stopped her. A glimmer, ever so slight, in the hem.

What's this?

Her finger ran over the edge and jumped at the feel of a solid object.

The glow became stronger.

Can it be?

She ripped the perfectly stitched edging and probed until she found the tiny, but very much active stone.

Eureka!

The first drops of precipitation splat against the wooden deck reminding her of the impending storm. She looked around unsure of how to protect the precious gem. As she thought about how best to safeguard the stone, she fingered the ever-present pendant around her neck. *Of course, the locket.*

Quickly, she uncoupled the latch and placed the opal inside. The snap of the closure reassured her the treasure was secure.

The clouds burst forth with pelting rain, but Rose hardly noticed. Her heart beat with excitement and her breath came in shallow gulps as she tried to contain her elation. *I'm getting off this blasted bucket of bolts. I'm anxious to see all their faces when I return.*

The blanket warmed her as she settled down to wait out the storm, and before long slumber overtook her. Dreams of freedom danced in her head, as did the dastardly deeds she meant to bestow on those who betrayed her. One hand gripped the pendant giving her comfort.

The night was lengthy, the watery assault unrelenting. She woke listening to the creak of the ship as the wind buffeted the ancient vessel to and fro. Somehow…this time, she wasn't afraid, soothed by the stone safely tucked away, ready to do her bidding.

Finally, dawn broke, and the rain stopped, but the gray clouds didn't promise a sunny day. Neither did the steady gale. The ship still rocked back and forth, keeping her off balance. But she let none of that disturb her elevated mood.

Carefully, she folded the blanket and replaced it inside the cupboard. She gave the coverlet a final pat and said, "Thank you."

It had been a long night and she was hungry. *First things first. I must renew my strength so I can think clearly how best to employ this great gift bestowed upon me.* She headed for the galley.

The rolls and jerky satisfied her hunger pains last night, but she was ready for a more substantial breakfast. *A celebratory meal. Just what I need.*

Hot coffee, scrambled eggs and bacon filled the bill. Renewed, she sat down at the table and gingerly opened the locket.

The gem twinkled at her, as if reassuring her of things to come.

She snapped the case closed. *How best can I utilize this gift? It's small and I have no idea how much capability it holds. How long will the strength last? And there bodes the question, how did this precious thing get inside the hem? I must be careful not to use the power until I know exactly what I can do with it.*

The galley comforted her with its warmth and the tantalizing smells of freshly cooked food, and of course, the nutty aroma of coffee. She poured another cup and thought about her next step.

I wonder who put that little opal there? A thought hit her like a bolt of lightning. *What if there are more of them? Tucked away in the blankets.*

She didn't finish the coffee but hurried up the stairs to the cabinet where she found the stone. In a frenzied motion, she threw the original blanket aside and examined the one below. Her fingers searched frantically along the hem, feeling for anything out of the ordinary. Once convinced nothing was hidden, she moved on to the next. One by one, she tossed them to the floor until she reached the bottom of the stack.

Nothing.

Disappointed, she ignored the pile of quilts strewn everywhere and made her way to the main deck. As she leaned against the railing, she thought hard about where another stone might be disguised. *The shaving mirror had one embedded in the glass. They used it to escape, but when I looked, it was gone.*

She determined there must be others on the ship. Chances are they held an opal.

The captain's cabin remained as they'd left it. The mirror still retained sentry in the corner. She ran a finger over the smooth surface, careful to cover every inch, but it was as before. Smooth, no opal to be found. *Okay, I had to double check. Now to look for more.*

Cabin by cabin, room by room, she searched for mirrors, even in the head at the front of the ship. She saw nothing.

Maybe there's a more creative way they've chosen to hide the gems. Say inside a book.

Once more in the captain's abode, she inspected his library. She'd played mind games with him when she hid the *Book of Spells* in plain sight to give him false hope. After thirty minutes of searching, she determined the book was not there.

"Barnacles," she whispered. "Wish I'd kept better track of that thing." She sighed. "Now what?"

Her brain hurt as she tried in the mortal way to solve the mystery. Reduced to human status without her own opal, she seethed with anger. *Blast! Where is the most likely place to hide something? You'd want it close at hand, not far from sight, but safely tucked away from prying eyes. Where would that be? Cecella isn't the queen because of her looks. She's crafty, cunning, a force to be reckoned with. Although she didn't interfere in what I did, she would have provided a method of rescue if one of my victims was shrewd enough. I have to think as she would.*

Several minutes passed, and a thought materialized.

The galley. It must be in there.

She tried to follow logic. The queen would want the captives to find it and where was the most populated space on the ship?

The coziest place here. The kitchen area.

In a frenzy, she tore through the cabinets, drawers, and every other container in the room. The vegetable bins, utensil drawers. About to give up, she spotted what looked like a small ornate carton the size of a match box tucked into a corner on the mug shelf. It was just above the stove and probably held only matches.

Very fancy for a box of matches, but just the kind of place someone might hide the stone. In plain sight.

She reached for it, fingered the fancy design on the top dulled by dust and age.

Her heart thumped in her chest.

As the ashy debris disappeared from the pewter box, an intricate weave of seaweed vines and cattails emerged around the edges in a charming crescent shape with marks shaped like waves intertwined.

But, what really caught her eye was the fin in the center. She looked closer and the mermaid came into focus. Long flowing hair, a beautiful face, and the graceful lines of a woman.

Her hands shook.

This is it.

Slowly, she slid the box open certain of what she would see.

However, nothing prepared her for what lay on the royal blue satin cloth inside.

CHAPTER THIRTY-FIVE

MAREN THOUGHT SHE COULDN'T LOVE DRAKE ANYMORE after his surprise reveal. He stood in the doorway yesterday in full uniform regalia, a magnificent specimen of masculinity, honor, and easily the most handsome man on the planet.

But here he stands, at the makeshift altar of spring flowers, and her breath caught. "I'm a lucky woman," she whispered.

Captain Henry Morgan nudged her. "Pardon? I didn't catch that."

"Nothing," she said, without tearing her gaze from her future husband. "Just look at him."

"He cuts quite a fine figure," Henry agreed.

Today was the first time she'd seen the full uniform, cap and all. When she'd asked about the headgear before, he'd smoothed the service dress coat with both hands and said, "You'll see the whole thing tomorrow night. I have to leave something to the imagination."

She took in the entire package now, a high stand-collar white tunic or 'choker', with shoulder boards showing his rank, white trousers, and white shoes. Various medals pinned on his chest boasted of his accomplishments. And on his head sat that cap... with the slightest tilt, oozing with his jaunty personality.

Captain Nelson wound his arm through hers and said, "It's time."

As he escorted her across the sand, music from the sea drifted within earshot. The mermaids and Queen Cecella sang a beautiful, haunting rendition of *Here Comes the Bride*.

Maren hardly recognized the tune, but then again, she did. Their own unique euphonious harmony was a perfect addition to their beach wedding.

As she and the captain approached Drake, she saw the twinkle in his eyes and smiled.

When she'd come to the seaside to work finding love never entered her thoughts, but now, life without Drake in it seemed impossible. In a short time, these two men became permanent fixtures in her life.

Her gaze fell on Telsa opposite Drake, glowing with happiness, dressed in the clothes she would wear for her travel back in time. Soft brown dress, with full petticoats. Somehow it suited her, even though she'd never seen her in such attire before. But her heart dropped as she realized time will separate them forever. *This is what she wants. How can I be sad? She's found love as I have.*

As they moved forward, she observed Nox standing between her groom and maid of honor. His slicked-back hair, the ill-fitting suit, his obvious discomfort made him an odd addition to the scene. But, as the mermaid's melody drifted over the water, she was glad they'd become friends.

At last, she arrived in front of Drake, ready to take the vows, eager for a new life. It was just the four of them, Nox, and the mermaids with the stars twinkling above while they announced their pledges to one another.

"You may kiss the bride," Nox said.

Drake drew her into his arms.

The kiss was warm, deep, yearning, and bursting with emotion. When they parted, Nox declared them man and wife.

Telsa and Henry hurried to their side and embraced them. "Congratulations, you two," Telsa said.

"May happiness follow you forever," Nelson added.

Nox approached and wished them well. "You'll forgive me if I excuse myself from the festivities. I'm needed back home."

She nodded. "Of course, Nox. Thank you for officiating. Please don't be a stranger. If you ever need us, you know where to find us."

He planted an awkward kiss on her cheek and shook Drake's hand. "I won't forget."

They watched as he disappeared into a thicket of trees, his bowed legs carrying him as fast as they could.

Maren realized they'd stared after him a bit too long. The mermaid's song was silent now and she knew the time had come for her friends to depart.

Queen Cecella moved closer and said, "I offer my deepest wish for you to be happy in your new union. I pray for long-lasting life for you both."

"Thank you, Queen, for all you've done for us. We might not be here, but for you," Maren said.

"I do not make a habit of interacting with mortals, but my assistance was needed. If you ever find trouble arrives because of the sea, call on me. I will come to your aid. But I warn you not to use that privilege lightly."

"Of course," Drake chimed in. "You have been most gracious, but might I ask, what is Rose's status? Can she come back to hurt us?"

"You need not worry about her. I've sent her a message to confirm her banishment is forever. Live your life without fear."

At their side, Telsa, pale and wide-eyed, and Henry, flushed, stood hand in hand.

Cecella turned her attention to them. "It is time."

The pair nodded.

Henry asked, "What would you like us to do?"

"The portal is on the other side of Passion Rock. Move to that side, the rest will take care of itself."

Telsa hugged Maren, then Drake. "Be happy."

Henry did the same. "Don't worry about us."

They clasped hands and without looking back walked to the rock. They stepped around the corner and out of sight.

Maren choked back a sob.

Drake held her tighter.

"No," she cried, and tried to run after them.

He pulled her back. "They're gone. Let it be."

She sobbed into his shoulder until the tears ran dry.

He murmured in her ear. "It's their time, whatever they choose to do with it. Remember today because it's also *our* time. We need to look forward, not back."

They stood alone under the midnight sky, united, pledged to live their lives together, to lean on each other, to help one another fulfill their dreams.

When she could control her emotions, she reached inside the pocket of her dress and removed an envelope. "Telsa left a letter for me."

He smiled and pulled one out of his own pocket. "So did Henry."

"Let's read them back at the cabin," she said.

They clasped hands and walked slowly to her place.

At the door, Drake lifted her in his arms to carry her over the threshold. As they entered, twinkling lights dazzled their eyes. Strands of them weaved in and out of every nook and cranny of the living room.

"Oh my gosh, how beautiful," she whispered. "When did they have time to do this?"

"Leave it to Telsa. She's so resourceful. What a wonderful thing to do," Drake echoed.

"Look, they lead to the bedroom."

He took her hand. "Then I think we should follow them."

Over the bed hung another brilliant display of twinkling lights, giving the room an enchanted ambience, filling Maren with joy at Telsa's gift to them.

"Let's sit and read our letters," Drake said. "You first."

She perched on the end of the bed, slid the envelope open, and removed the letter.

'Dear Maren,

We've known each other a long time and I will always carry you in my heart. So on this day, I want only happiness for you and Drake. You deserve it. Don't worry about me. Henry will be my protector in the new land. Concentrate on your lives together. Keep a prayer in your heart for our safety and happiness as we seek this new life. Continue your journey in this newest endeavor as publisher, but don't forget to also pursue your passion as an illustrator.

Maybe you can find a bookstore close by that will give you some historical information about us, who knows. At any rate, don't be sad. This is what I want.

With love always in my heart for the best friend a gal can have,
Affection,
Telsa'

Tears dripped from her cheeks and splashed on the letter, smearing a bit of the ink. She quickly dabbed the letter with a corner of her dress.

"My turn," Drake said.

'My dear friend,

I almost hesitate to address you as friend because you are so much more to me, and I really feel we are related somehow. I hope you can do the research there in your time to find the connection.

Thank you for all your help, getting us off the ship, loaning me clothes, introducing me to new foods and drink. It's a time I will cherish always.

Take care of that lovely bride. She's a keeper for sure. I know you two will be very happy. When you look out at the sea, picture Telsa and I together finding happiness in this new world. I feel in my bones we will cross paths again someday.

Keep us in your prayers, as you will always be in ours.
With respect and affection,
Captain Henry Nelson

CHAPTER THIRTY-SIX

THE NEXT FEW DAYS FOR MAREN LIVED UP TO EVERYTHING she ever dreamed of in a honeymoon; time alone with Drake, talking about their future, making love, and walking hand in hand on the beach. On the third day, they spoke to a realtor and arranged to purchase Maren's rented cabin. A dream home was in their future, but for now, they were content.

Drake's sabbatical from the yacht touring business closed in on them, so they took some time to run into town to enjoy a nice lunch and get to know the village a little better before returning to work as usual. She looked forward to working remotely.

They decided on a leisurely stroll and, hand in hand, set out to find a local bistro they'd heard about.

Halfway into town, her red-headed neighbor, Josh, walked toward them, squinting, shaking his head. He shouted as he approached, "Maren, is that really you? My gosh, where have you been? Everyone's been looking for you."

She hugged his neck and said, "I know, Josh. Let's just say I took a little unexpected trip. I didn't mean to cause anyone concern. I'm back now and married." She beamed at her new husband.

"Married? Wow, didn't expect that." He stammered a moment, then said, "But congrats to you both. You probably need to let the police know you've returned. They think something suspicious happened. Will you be heading back to Seattle?"

"No, as a matter of fact, we bought the cabin I'm in, for now, anyway. I'm going to work from here," she explained. She paused to look up at Drake. "We should stop by the police station."

He nodded.

Josh offered his hand. "Let's have a celebratory fish fry at your convenience. Everyone will want to congratulate you." The men shook, then he hugged Maren. "Let me know when there's a good time for you. And really, I wish you all the happiness."

"Thanks, friend," Maren said.

They watched Josh trudge toward his own cabin, then turned back to the village.

"Nice of Josh to offer the fish fry," Maren said.

"I'm always up for free food," Drake agreed.

The little village wasn't too busy. A few people wandered about, and Maren suspected they were tourists.

"Do you see the police station anywhere?"

He glanced around. "Nope. But it can't be far. I see the bistro across the street. They can tell us." He squeezed her hand and smiled down at her.

Pleased, she squeezed back and prepared to cross the street, but stopped short. "Look, a bookstore. How quaint. I've never noticed it before. Let's go in for a minute."

"Sure, let's go. I love the name, *The Last Chapter*." He followed her inside.

The little bell tinkled over the door and the smell of leather hit her nostrils. "Oh my, this bookstore carries some old vintages. This is what a bookstore *should* smell like." She sniffed the aroma of old books and leather. Roses in every corner brightened the interior.

A female voice from the back called out, "I'll be right with you."

"No hurry," Maren replied. "We love to browse." She pulled Drake toward the section marked *History*. "You know, we might find something referencing the time Henry and Telsa went back to. Wouldn't that be wonderful?"

"Looks like there is quite a bit here. You take halfway down; I'll tackle the top."

Engrossed in their search, they didn't hear the attendant approach behind them.

"Looking for something specific?" she said.

Maren turned. "Yes, we…" She broke off and stared at the woman.

Drake pulled a book from the top shelf, turned to his bride, and said, "I think I found…"

He also stopped in mid-sentence.

"Is something wrong? You look as though you've seen a ghost," the woman said.

Maren couldn't speak. She was staring into the eyes of her beloved friend, Telsa. The same glossy black hair, those aster blue eyes. Her words, hoarse and emotional, came haltingly. "How… did you get here?"

"I beg your pardon? I've lived here all my life. I've never seen you two before. Are you tourists?" the Telsa look-a-like said.

"Yes, er, I mean no. We…just got married. We live up the beach." Sans ceremony, she blurted, "What's your name?"

"Well, if you must know, it's Doris. Named after my grandmother who loved the sea. That's what it means. 'The sea'. You look positively shocked. Please tell me what's wrong."

Instead of answering Doris's question, she asked another. "What's your last name?"

"Look, you're freaking me out. Why all the questions? Did you come in to buy a book or what?"

Drake came forward and reached out his hand. "I'm Drake and this is my wife, Maren. We're newlyweds." He grinned. "It's just that you look so much like someone we know, er, used to know. You could be her twin."

"Really?"

"Please, what is your last name?" Maren insisted.

"Nelson. Come from a long line of Nelson's."

Maren's knees buckled.

Drake caught her before she hit the floor, then said, "Henry Nelson? Wife, Telsa?"

"My forebears as it were, how did you know?"

Maren looked at Drake. "How can it be?"

He shook his head and didn't answer.

"It's difficult to explain. I'm familiar with both your great-grandparents. Or great-great, as the case may be. I, well, I studied them. Their journey, so to speak," Maren said.

Doris's blue eyes widened. "What did you say your last name was?"

"I didn't, but it's Morgan now," she answered.

"No, before. What was it before you married?"

"Raybourn. Maren Raybourn."

This time Doris paled as if *she'd* seen the ghost. "My God, it's happened."

"What's happened?"

"You've come." She turned toward the back room, then spun around to face them. "Wait, I'll be right back."

Drake moved closer to Maren and took her hand. "Can it be? Is she a descendant of Telsa and Henry's?"

"She looks exactly like Telsa. I thought it was her, at first."

Doris returned holding an old wooden box. She tried to dust it off and sneezed as the powdered flakes floated into the air. "Sorry, it's been a long time since it was moved. My grandmother handed it down to me. She got it from her mother. It was never to be opened except by the person it was intended for, a Maren Raybourn. That must be you."

"Don't you want to make sure I'm the right person?"

"Grandmother said I'd know. I'd just know. And judging by your reactions today, I'd say you are the correct Maren Raybourn."

Maren gingerly reached for the box. The object was secured with a small brass hasp latch with a tiny padlock. "How can we open it? I don't want to break the lock."

"Oh, just a moment. I forgot. There's a key." Doris returned to the back room.

"Look at the carving on the top, Drake. If you look closely, you can see Telsa's and Henry's initials intertwined with their last name." Maren ran her finger over the scrolling.

"It's beautiful," Drake whispered.

Doris returned with the tiniest of keys and handed it to Maren. "I've kept this locked in my safe for years. Sometimes, I wonder how my ancestors managed to hold on to it, the key is so small."

Maren set the box on the counter and inserted the key, turned it, and watched as the lock sprung as if brand new. Carefully, she slid out the lock and lifted the hasp. The first thing she saw was Telsa's handwriting on an envelope. She'd know it anywhere and opened it with care.

My dear, Maren,

If you find this then my wish has come true. That I can let you know, Henry and I are fine, happy, living the life we dreamed of when we left you. I have two healthy sons and a daughter. We are about to become grandparents. I should have written about our life sooner, but we were busy raising our family. I knew it would be centuries before this letter would find its way to you. I pray my descendants have honored my wishes and kept this safe. Of course, if you are reading this, we are long dead, but our legacy will live on in our children, grandchildren, and great- grandchildren. If you have the good fortune to meet one of them take good care and make friends with them. That way you will have a piece of me with you.

I made the right choice, Maren. I've had a full and happy life. Do not mourn for me. Embrace my descendant. Tell them about our life together and why I chose to go back in time with Henry.

I pray you and Drake found happiness together. I think of you often and wonder about your life. Miss you, dear friend.

Always in my heart, Telsa

CHAPTER THIRTY-SEVEN

D RAKE WATCHED THE TEARS STREAM DOWN MAREN'S CHEEKS and smiled. He understood they were tears of joy as she read the age-old letter to the others. "See, you had nothing to worry about. They were happy."

"I know," she said, smoothing the parchment carefully. "It's just that …they're …dead. It's hard to fathom."

He glanced at Doris's face dark with confusion. "It's a long story," he explained. "It will take some time for you to understand."

"You…knew them? My great-grandparents? I've heard the stories, but never thought they were true," Doris said.

The perplexed look on her face deepened. "Look, we can't talk about this while your shop is open for business. You must hear this without interruption. Even then, I'm afraid you might not believe it," Drake said.

Doris marched over to the door, locked it, and turned the open sign to closed. "You will tell me now. I've been waiting for years to find someone who knows about the stories I was told as a child. I have a small break room in the back. Join me. I'll make coffee."

"If you're sure," Maren said.

Doris nodded. "I'm sure. Come with me." She turned toward the break room but stopped at Maren's exclamation.

"Wait, there's something more in the box. A piece of blue cloth." She removed the bundle, carefully.

"It's a wrapping of sorts," he said, and moved closer for a better look.

She removed the cloth and stared. "A stone. A blue opal." Drake looked closer.

Silence filled the room at the sight of the unusual stone, shards of light bounced off the gem, illuminated by the overhead light. The display gave the room an ethereal feel.

"A blue Peruvian opal?" Drake asked.

Maren's voice turned reverent as she declared, "A blue glow. It's beautiful."

"Protection. A blue opal is for protection and luck," Doris whispered.

"How do you know?" Maren looked up and asked.

Doris's voice trembled. "My grandmother taught me about gemstones and their meanings and uses. She was a great believer in their power. She always mentioned them in the stories she told."

"She's right. I had a captain one time who believed in their power. Taught me all about them," Drake agreed.

"But why would she give this to us?" Maren asked.

He bent to look inside the box. "Is there more inside?"

She examined the bottom of the box and pulled out another piece of paper. Telsa's handwriting jumped off the page.

We never needed the stone. Henry's family insisted we keep it for protection after they heard our story. Rose never appeared in our time. Henry and I are afraid Rose might take vengeance on you if she were somehow to become free. Keep this with you.

"You speak of someone called Rose. The stories handed down tell of an evil mermaid with that name. She steals souls so she can live on land. Is it the same one?" Doris asked.

"I believe so. She wanted Drake as her own and tried to

steal my soul to achieve her goal." She looked up at Drake. "He rescued me."

Doris gave a weak smile. "May I ask how long ago you saw my great-grandparents?"

Drake glanced at Maren first, knowing the truth would be hard for Doris to accept.

Maren nodded and encouraged him to tell her.

"Three days ago…at our wedding. They stood up for us as witnesses," he explained.

Doris choked out the words. "Three days…how is that possible? They've been dead over two hundred years."

He patted her on the shoulder. "Let's have our coffee. We'll tell you everything."

Doris busied herself with coffee-making as Drake and Maren found their chairs around the antique break table, heavy wood polished to a shine. The chairs, equally as heavy, made a scraping sound as they moved them out to sit.

"Beautiful table," Maren noted.

Doris let her gaze rest on the table for a moment. "Thank you. Handed down from my grandmother. Who knows, maybe Telsa sat at this very table back in the day."

Once the cups were filled and Doris sat down across from them, she said. "Okay, tell me all of it."

Over the next hour, Drake explained the entire story to the bookstore owner who sat enraptured at the tale.

"So, that's it," he said. "I'm sure you have questions."

Doris sat back. "No, I have no questions. You told the story exactly as my grandmother told me. I can see it unfolding just as you said. Although the whole time-travel is hard to fathom. How can they have been here three days ago, yet died so long ago? It boggles the mind."

"We're still trying to wrap our heads around it, too," Maren agreed.

"Do you think Rose will come back?" Doris asked.

"We were assured by Queen Cecella she will not. But Rose is wily. If there's a way to free herself, she'll find it. I only pray she does not," Maren said. In a quiet voice, she continued, "I wish you could meet the queen. She's lovely, and so kind."

"Oh, I'd like that. How does one go about meeting this Queen?"

Maren smiled. "She can be summoned, but one can't abuse the privilege. Has to be a borderline emergency."

Drake interjected, "I think we might be able to arrange it. After all, I would assess this as an emergency. Doris is a descendant of Telsa's. Maybe she can explain the time-travel issue."

Doris looked from one to the other with a hopeful countenance.

Maren glanced around the room. "How long have you had this bookstore? I never noticed it before, although I haven't been to town much."

"Oh." The light went out of her eyes. "This store has been here since I can remember. My mother ran it before me. Her mother before her."

Maren nodded. "Explains the old vintage aroma in here. I love the smell of old books."

Drake interrupted the change of topic. "Maren, Doris deserves to meet Cecella. She's the one instrumental in sending Telsa and Henry back. I suggest we do a midnight rendezvous with the queen tonight. The worst-case scenario is she doesn't show."

"You're right, of course. I only hope we don't summon her on a whim. Use up our good will with her," Maren said.

Drake added, "I don't think this constitutes a whim. Doris is important in this whole scenario. She might also be an ally when it comes to Rose."

"I don't want to cause any problems," Doris said.

"No problem. Drake is right. Can you meet on the beach at Passion Rock at midnight?" Maren asked.

Doris's face lit up. "Yes, absolutely."

"Good," Drake said. "Now we have to clear something up at the police station."

He pulled Maren to her feet. "Let's go. Doris, we'll see you at midnight."

As Maren walked hand in hand with Drake, she said, "The police sure were understanding about my disappearance. I don't mind doing a bit of community service to repay them for the investigation. They bought the story that I needed time to think about my feelings toward you. I don't think it's wise to relay the real story about the mermaids."

"You're right, no need to feed their imagination when it comes to Rose," Drake commented. "I had to laugh when they tried to explain about Rose disappearing right in front of them. You were genius when you asked, 'Rose who'? And you didn't know any person by that name. They dropped the subject real quick."

"What about her cabin? She did occupy it for a time. It can't just stand empty full of her belongings. Someone will notice," Maren continued.

"I thought of it a while ago. I already checked with the realtor. She has no record of anyone named Rose ever being in that cabin. It's as if she was never there."

"An after effect of time travel, maybe?" Maren asked.

"Could be."

They held hands on the way back to their cabin, occasionally stealing a kiss, content, happy, and very much in love.

Midnight approached and Maren woke Drake gently. "Time to go," she whispered.

They pulled on matching plaid jackets and made the short trip to Passion Rock only to find Doris already there, an eagerness on her face as they came into view.

"Are you ready for this?" Maren asked.

"Oh yes," the bookstore owner replied. Her blue eyes danced in the moonlight.

Maren saw her shiver, not knowing if it was from the chill of the evening or excitement.

Drake stood beside her at the edge of the water.

The stars twinkled across the ocean in a splendorous light show.

Maren faced the water and called out, "Queen Cecella we summon you. We discovered a new friend today. Will you grace us with your presence?"

At first, the sea remained calm, but after a few minutes, a song broke through the silence getting louder as it approached the threesome.

"It's her," Maren whispered, the familiar tremble at the sight radiated through her body.

Behind the queen, a chorus of mermaids sang a lilting song.

Doris stood open-mouthed at the sight.

"You summoned me?" the queen asked.

"Yes, this is Doris Nelson, descendant of Telsa and Henry. She wanted to meet you," she continued.

Queen Cecella smiled at the woman.

"You knew my great-grandmother and were responsible for sending her back in time?" Doris blurted.

"Yes, my child."

"Can you tell me about them? How is it even possible?"

Maren squeezed Drake's hand. "I think this is a conversation they need to have in private. Let's go back to the cabin."

Maren looked back over her shoulder as Cecella and Doris conversed, happy she was getting a few answers. "I haven't lost Telsa, after all, Drake. She's right here in Doris. I am sure we will be fast friends."

"Yes, in a way, we should thank Rose for bringing us together. We're going to have a wonderful life here," he answered. "I love you so much."

EPILOGUE

ROSE HELD THE SMALL PEWTER BOX IN HER HAND AND stared at the object nestled in the velvet lining.

It's meaning was clear.

A miniature timepiece, the face cracked, with no hands to keep time. Below the tiny clock, perfectly placed, were two tiny bird bones in the sign of an X.

Blood pounded in her ears, the thud of her heart knocked against her chest, and beads of perspiration dotted her forehead.

The Queen only sends this message as a final pronouncement. All efforts to find a way off this ship are doomed.

She snapped the lid shut and tried to catch her breath. *She can curse me all she wants, but I will not give up. I found one small gem. I'll keep searching for others so I can gain power.*

After she placed the box back on the shelf, she studied it. Her eyes, squeezed into mere slits, glowed with evil. Her voice became a low snarl. *I'm going to keep it in sight as a reminder to steady my resolve. I'm not beaten yet. We'll see whose power will win this race!*

A twisted smile settled on her lips as she left the galley.

When she emerged from below the wind caught her hair, lifting it into a wild tangle around her face. The brisk air heightened her senses, making her giddy. From the depths of her soul unfettered laughter bubbled up until it erupted into a primitive cackle.

"I'll find a way," she shouted into the whirlwind. "You haven't beaten me yet!"

ACKNOWLEDGEMENTS

Many have helped me with this endeavor.

My critique partners, Ruth Buck, Dana Wayne, Beth Howlett, Phyllis A. Still, Ginger Arnold.

My cover artist Tina Iliff

My wonderful granddaughter, Savannah Cameron, the model for the cover.

My publisher Susan Reeder.

My husband who makes sure I live my dream, Ron Wiseman.

To all of you who encourage me, support me, and lift me up, thank you!

ABOUT THE AUTHOR

 Author Patty Wiseman is a native of Seattle, Washington area. She moved to Bartlesville, Oklahoma after high school to attend The Wesleyan College. After college she moved to Northeast Texas, where she met and married her Texas born husband, Ron.

Her two sons are grown and pursuing their own dreams.

After a twenty-five-year career as an administrative assistant to a financial professional, she retired, and is finally living her dream. She has settled into the writing life with gusto. Eleven books are published, and she is still writing. She's accumulated multiple awards and enjoys mentoring new writers. An avid history buff with a weakness for a good riddle, her books will keep you riveted as you try to solve the mysteries and are swept away with the romance.

A special treat is having her granddaughter, Savannah Cameron featured on the cover of two of her books.

Favorite quote "Find out who you are, then do it on purpose."
~ Dolly Parton

www.ingramcontent.com/pod-product-compliance
Lightning Source LLC
Chambersburg PA
CBHW051306210726

48287CB00002B/701